"A DELICATE SITUATION," MAJOR LORCA SAID

"We cannot hold the city without supply, and we cannot supply the city without keeping the river transport lines open. In the past, Governor Swale and Colonel Harrington were agreed that the only way to do that was to extend CoDominium rule to these areas along the river." The light pointer moved, indicating the area marked as held by the River Pack.

"They resisted us," Lorca said. "Not only the convicts, but the original colonists as well. Our convoys were attacked. Our militiamen were shot down by snipers. Bombs were thrown into the homes of militia officers—the hostiles don't have many sympathizers inside the city, but it doesn't take many to employ terror tactics."

"They beat our arses," Harrington said to Falkenberg. His lips were tightly drawn. "We had to send back to Headquarters for Marine reinforcements. I asked for a destroyer and a regiment of military police. The warship and the Marines would have taken the goddam riverbanks, and the M.P.'s could hold it for us. Instead, I got you people."

JERRY POURNELLE

WEST OF HONOR

BAEN BOOKS

WEST OF HONOR

A Baen Book

Baen Publishing Enterprises
260 Fifth Avenue
New York, N.Y. 10001

First Baen printing, August 1987

ISBN: 0-671-65347-4

Cover art by Wayne Barlowe

Printed in the United States of America

Distributed by
SIMON & SCHUSTER
1230 Avenue of the Americas
New York, N.Y. 10020

To junior officers
everywhere

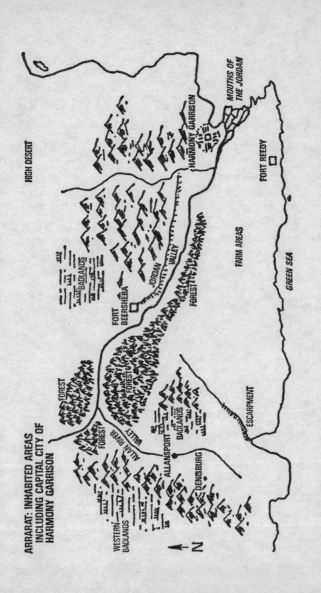

ARRARAT: INHABITED AREAS
INCLUDING CAPITAL CITY OF
HARMONY GARRISON

Chronology

1969   Neil Armstrong sets foot on Earth's moon.

1990   Series of treaties between the United States and Soviet Union creates the CoDominium. Military research and development outlawed.

1996   French Foreign Legion transferred to CoDominium control to form the basic element of the CD Armed Services.

2004   Alderson Drive is perfected at Cal Tech.

2006   Ban on military research extended.

2008   First Alderson Drive exploratory ships leave the solar system for other stars.

2010   Habitable planets discovered in other star systems. Commercial exploitation begins. CD Intelligence licenses all scientists and begins censorship of scientific publications.

2020   First interstellar colonies founded. CoDominium Space Navy created. Great Exodus begins as adventurous leave Earth to settle on other planets.

2031   CoDominium Navy absorbs all other CD Armed Services.

2040   CoDominium Bureau of Relocation (BuRelock) begins mass outsystem shipment of involuntary colonists.

2043   John Christian Falkenberg is born in Rome.

PROLOGUE

2064 A.D.

The bright future she sang of was already stiffened in blood, but Kathryn Malcolm didn't know that, any more than she knew that the sun was orange-red and too bright, or that the gravity was too low.

She had lived all of her sixteen standard years on Arrarat, and although her grandfather often spoke of Earth, humanity's birthplace was no home to her. Earth was a place of machines and concrete roads and automobiles and great cities, a place where people crowded together far from the land. When she thought of Earth at all, it seemed an ugly place, hardly fit for people to live on.

Mostly she wondered how Earth would smell. With all those people huddled together—certainly it must be different from Arrarat. She inhaled deeply, filling her lungs with the pleasing smell of newly turned soil. The land here was good. It felt right beneath her feet. Dark and crumbly, moist enough to take hold of the seeds and nurture them, but not wet and

1

full of clods: good land, perfect land for the late-season crop she was planting.

She walked steadily behind the plow, using a long whip to guide the oxen. She flicked the whip near the leaders, but never close enough to touch them. There was no need for that. Horace and Star knew what she wanted. The whip guided them and assured them that she was watching, but they knew the spiral path as well as she did. The plow turned the soil inward so that the center of the field would be higher than the edges. That helped to drain the field and made it easier to harvest two crops each year.

The early harvest was already gathered into the stone barn. Wheat and corn, genetically adapted for Arrarat; and in another part of the barn were Arrarat's native breadfruit melons, full of sugar and ready to begin fermentation. It had been a good year, with more than enough for the family to eat. There would be a surplus to sell in town, and Kathryn's mother had promised to buy a bolt of printed cloth for a new dress that Kathryn could wear for Emil.

At the moment, though, she wore coveralls and high boots, and she was glad enough that Emil couldn't see her. He should know that she could plow as straight a furrow as any man, and that she could ride as well as her brother—but knowing it and seeing her here on the fields were two different things entirely, and she was glad that he couldn't see her just now. She laughed at herself when she thought this, but that didn't stop the thoughts.

She twitched the whip to move the oxen slightly outward, then frowned imperceptibly. The second pair in the string had never pulled a wagon across the plains, and Kathryn thought that she could no longer put off their training. Emil would not want to live with Kathryn's grandfather. A man wanted land of his own, even though there were more than a thousand hectares in the Malcolm station.

The land here was taken. If she and Emil were to have land of their own, they would have to move westward, toward the other sea, where the satellite pictures showed good land. We could go, she thought; go so far that the convicts will never find us, and the city will be a place to see once in a lifetime. It would be exciting, although she would hate to leave this valley.

The field she plowed lay among low hills. A small stream meandered along one edge. Most of the crops and trees that she could see had come from Earth as seeds, and they had few predators. Most crop eaters left Earth plants alone, especially if the fields were bordered with spearmints and marigolds to give off odors that even Earth insects detested.

She thought of what she would need if they struck west to found a new settlement. Seeds they would have; and a mare and stallion, and two pairs of oxen; chickens and swine; her grandfather was rich by local standards. There would be her father's blacksmithing tools, which Emil could learn to use.

They would need a television. Those were rare. A television, and solar cells, and a generator for the windmill; such manufactured goods had to be bought in the city, and that took money. The second crop would be needed this year, and a large one next spring, as well—and they would have to keep all the money they earned. She thrust that thought away, but her hand strayed toward the big sheath knife she wore on her belt.

We will manage, she thought. We will find the money. Children should not go without education. Television was not for entertainment. The programs relayed by the satellites gave weather reports and taught farming, ecology, engineering, metalwork—all the skills needed to live on Arrarat. They also taught reading and mathematics. Most of Kathryn's neighbors despised television and wouldn't have it in their houses, but their children had to learn from others who watched the screen.

And yet, Kathryn thought, there is cause for concern. First it is television. Then light industry. Soon there is more. Mines are opened. Larger factories are built, and around them grow cities. She thought of Arrarat covered with cities and concrete, the animals replaced by tractors and automobiles, the small villages grown into cities; people packed together the way they were in Harmony and Garrison; streams dammed and lakes dirty with sewage; and she shuddered. Not in my time, or my grandchildren's. And perhaps we will be smarter than they were on Earth, and it will never happen here. We know better now. We know how to live with the land.

Her grandfather had been a volunteer colonist, an engineer with enough money to bring tools and equipment to Arrarat, and he was trying to show others how to live with technology. He had a windmill for electricity. It furnished power for the television and the radio. He had radio communications with Denisburg, forty kilometers away, and although the neighbors said they despised all technology, they were not too proud to ask Amos Malcolm to send messages for them.

The Malcolm farm had running water and an efficient system for converting sewage to fertilizer. To Amos, technology was something to be used so long as it did not use you, and he tried to teach his neighbors that.

The phone buzzed to interrupt her thoughts, and Kathryn halted the team. The phone was in the center of the plowed land, where it was plugged into a portable solar reflector that kept its batteries charged.

There were very few radio-phones in the valley. They cost a great deal and could only be bought in Harmony. Even her grandfather Amos couldn't manufacture the phone's microcircuits, although he often muttered about buying the proper tools and making something that would be as good. "After all," he was fond of saying, "we do not need the very latest. Only something that will do."

Before she reached the phone, she heard the gunshots. They sounded far away, but they came from the direction of her home. She looked toward the hill that hid the ranch from her, and a red trail streaked skyward. It exploded in a cloud of bright smoke. Amos had sent up a distress rocket. "God, no!" Kathryn screamed. She ran for the phone, but she dropped it in her haste. She scrabbled it up from the freshly plowed dirt and shouted into it. "Yes!"

"Go straight to the village, child," her grandfather's voice told her. He sounded very old and tired. "Do not come home. Go quickly."

"Grandfather—"

"Do as I say! The neighbors will come, and you cannot help."

"But—"

"Kathryn." He spoke urgently, but there were centuries in the voice. "They are here. Many of them."

"Who?" she demanded.

"Convicts. They claim to be sheriffs, executing a writ for collection of taxes. I will not pay. My house is strong, Kathryn, and the neighbors will come. The convicts will not get in, and if they kill me now it is no great matter—"

"And mother!" Kathryn shouted.

"They will not take her alive," Amos Malcolm said. "We have talked of this, and you know what I will do. Please. Do not make my whole life meaningless by letting them get you as well. Go to the village, and God go with you. I must fight now."

There were more sounds of firing in the distance. The phone was silent. Then there were rifle shots, plus the harsh stammer of a machine gun. Amos had good defenses for his stone ranch house.

Kathryn heard grenades, sharp explosions, but not loud, and she prayed that she would not hear the final explosion that meant Amos had set off the dynamite under his house. He had often sworn that before he would let anyone take his home, he would blow it and them to hell.

Kathryn ran back to unhitch the oxen. They would be safe enough. The sounds of firing would keep them from going home until the next day, and here on the plains there were no animals large enough to be a threat to healthy oxen. None except men.

She left the team standing beside the plow, their eyes puzzled because the sun was high and the field was not yet plowed, and she ran to the shade trees by the creek. A horse and dog waited patiently there. The dog jumped up playfully, but he sank onto the ground and cringed as he sensed her mood.

Kathryn hurled the saddle onto the horse and fumbled with the leather straps. Her hands were moving so quickly that even familiar motions were difficult, and she was clumsy in her haste. She tied the phone and solar reflector in place behind the saddle and mounted. There was a rifle in the saddle scabbard, and she took it out and fingered it longingly.

Then she hesitated. The guns were still firing. She still heard her grandfather's machine gun and more grenades, and that meant that Amos was alive. *I should help*, she thought. *I should go*.

Emil will be there. He was to plow the field next to our boundary, and he will have heard. He will be there. She turned the horse toward the ranch.

One rider can do no good, she realized. But though she knew that, she knew she must go to her home before it was too late. They would have a good chance, Emil and her grandfather. The house was strong, made of good stone, low to the ground, much of it buried in the earth, sod roof above waterproof plastic. It would withstand raiders. It had before, many times, but there were very many rifles firing now and she could not remember that large a raid before. Not here, and not anywhere.

The phone buzzed again. "Yes!" she shouted. "What is happening?"

"Ride, girl! Ride! Do not disobey my last command. You are all I have—" The voice broke off before Amos said more, and Kathryn held the silent phone and stared at it.

"All I have," Amos had said. Her mother and her brother were dead, then.

She screamed words of hatred and rode toward the sound of the guns. As she crossed over the creek she heard mortars firing, then louder explosions.

Two hundred riders converged on the Malcolm ranch. They rode hard, their horses drenched in sweat, and they came by families, some with their women, all with their oldest boys. Brown dogs ran ahead of them. Their panting tongues hung out between bared fangs as the dogs sensed the anger their masters projected. As the families of riders saw each other, they waved and kicked their horses into an even faster pace.

The riders approached the final rise before the Malcolm ranch and slowed to a trot. There were no sounds from over the hill. Shouted commands sent the dogs ahead. When the loping brown forms went over the hill without halting, the riders kicked their horses back to the gallop and rode on.

"He didn't use the dynamite," George Woodrow said. "I heard explosions, but not Amos's magazines." His neighbors didn't answer. They rode down the hill toward the ranch house.

There was the smell of explosives in the air, mixed with the bright copper smell of fresh blood. The dogs loped among dead men who lay around the stone house. The big front door stood open, and more dead lay in front of that. A girl in bloodstained coveralls and muddy boots sat in the dirt by the open door. She cradled a boy's head in her arms. She rocked gently, not aware of the motion, and her eyes were dry and bright.

"My God!" George Woodrow shouted. He dismounted and knelt beside her. His hand reached out toward the boy, but he couldn't touch him. "Kathryn—"

"They're all dead," Kathryn said. "Grandfather, mother, my brother, and Emil. They're all dead." She spoke calmly, telling George Woodrow of his son's death as she might tell him that there would be a dance at the church next Saturday.

George looked at his dead son and the girl who would have borne his grandchildren. Then he stood and leaned his face against his saddle. He remained that way for a long time. Gradually he became aware that others were talking.

"—caught them all outside except Amos," Harry Seeton said. He kept his voice low, hoping that Kathryn and George Woodrow wouldn't hear. "I think Amos shot Jeanine after they'd grabbed her. How in hell did anyone sneak up on old Amos?"

"Found a dog with an arrow in him back there," Wan Loo said. "A crossbow bolt. Perhaps that is how."

"I still don't understand it," Seeton insisted.

"Go after them!" Kathryn stood beside her dead fiancé. "Ride!"

"We will ride," Wan Loo said. "When it is time."

"Ride now!" Kathryn demanded.

"No." Harry Seeton shook his head sadly. "Do you think this was the only place raided today? A dozen more. Most did not even fight. There are hundreds more raiders, and they will have joined together by now. We cannot ride until there are more of us."

"And then what?" George Woodrow asked. His voice was bitter. "By the time there are enough of us, they will be in the hills again." He looked helplessly at the line of high foothills just at the horizon. "God! Why?"

"Do not blaspheme." The voice was strident. Roger Dornan wore dark clothing, and his face was lean and narrow. *He looks like an undertaker*, Kathryn thought. "The ways of the Lord are not to be questioned," Dornan intoned.

"We don't need that talk, Brother Dornan," Kathryn said. "We need revenge! I thought we had *men* here! George, will you ride with me to hunt your son's murderer?"

"Put your trust in the Lord," Dornan said. "Lay this burden on His shoulders."

"I cannot allow you to ride," Wan Loo said. "You and George would be killed, and for what? You gain no revenge by throwing yourself at their guns." He motioned, and two of his sons went to hold Kathryn's horse. Another took George Woodrow's mount and led it away. "We need all our farmers," Wan Loo said. "And what would become of George's other children? And his wife with the unborn child? You cannot go."

"Got a live one," a rider called. Two men lifted a still figure from the ground. They carried him over to where the others had gathered around Kathryn and George Woodrow, then dropped him into the dirt. Wan Loo knelt and felt for the pulse. Then he seized the raider's hair and lifted the head. Methodically he slapped the face. His fingers left vivid red marks on the too-white flesh. Smack, smack! Forehand, backhand, methodically, and the raider's head rocked with each blow.

"He's about gone," Harry Seeton said.

"All the more reason he should be awakened," Wan Loo said. He ignored the spreading bloodstains on the raider's leather jacket, and turned him face down into the dirt. He seized an arm and twisted violently. The raider grunted.

The raider was no older than twenty. He had a short scraggly beard, not well developed. He wore dark trousers and a leather jacket and soft leather boots much like Kathryn's. There were marks on his fingers, discolorations where rings had been, and his left earlobe was torn.

"They stripped their own dead and wounded," Woodrow grunted. "What all did they get?"

"The windmill generator," Harry Seeton reported. "And all the livestock, and some of the electronics. The phone's gone, too. Wonder why Amos didn't blow the place?"

"Shaped charge penetrated the wall," one of the riders said. "Killed Amos at his gun."

"Leggo. Stop." The young raider moaned. "That hurts."

"He is coming awake," Wan Loo told them. "But he will not last long."

"Pity," George Woodrow said. He bent down and slapped the boy's face. "Wake up, damn you! I want you to feel the rope around your neck! Harry, get a rope."

"You must not," Brother Dornan said. "Vengeance is the Lord's—"

"We'll just help the Lord out a bit," Woodrow said. "Get a rope!"

"Yeah," Seeton said. "I guess. Kathryn?"

"Get it. Give it to me. I want to put it around his neck." She looked down at the raider. "Why?" she demanded. "Why?"

For a moment the boy's eyes met hers. "Why not?"

Three men dug graves on the knoll above the valley. Kathryn came up the hill silently, and they did not see her at first. When they did they stopped working, but she said nothing, and after a while they dug again. Their shovels bit into the rich soil.

"You're digging too many graves," Kathryn said. "Fill one in."

"But—"

"My grandfather will not be buried here," Kathryn said.

The men stopped digging. They looked at the girl and her bloodstained coveralls, then glanced out at the horizon where the rest of the commandos had gone. There was dust out there. The riders were coming home. They wouldn't have caught the raiders before they went into the hills.

One of the gravediggers made a silent decision. Next spring he would take his family and find new lands. It would be better than this. But he wondered if the convicts would not follow wherever he went. When men work the earth, others will come to kill and steal.

"Where?" he asked finally.

"Bury Amos in his doorway," Kathryn said.

"That is a terrible thing, to bury a man in his own door. He will not rest—"

"I don't want him to rest," Kathryn said. "I want him to walk! I want him to walk and remind us all of what Earth has done to us!"

ONE

"Hear this. All hands brace for re-entry. Hear this."

"Seat straps, Lieutenant," Sergeant Cernan said.

"Right." I pulled the shoulder straps down into place and latched them, then looked out at Arrarat.

The planet had a bleak look, not like Earth. There were few clouds, and lots of desert. There were also heavy jungle forests near the equator. The only cultivated lands I could see were on a narrow strip at the northern edge of a nearly land-locked sea. South of the sea was another continent. It looked dry and dusty, desert land where men had left no mark in passing—if anyone had ever been there at all.

Northward and westward from the cultivated strip were hills and forests, high desert plateaus, high mountains, and ragged canyons. There were streaks through the forests and across the hills, narrow roads not much more than tracks. When the troopship got lower I could see villages and towns, and every one of them had walls or a stockade and ditch. They looked like tiny fortresses.

The ship circled until it had lost enough speed to

make a landing approach. Then it ran eastward, and we could see the city. My briefing folio said it was the only city on Arrarat. It stood on a high bluff above the sea, and it seemed huddled in on itself. It looked like a medieval walled town, but it was made of modern concrete, and adobe with plastic waterproofing, and other materials medieval craftsmen probably wouldn't have used if they'd had them.

As the ship passed over the city at two thousand meters, it became obvious that there were really two cities run together, with only a wall between them. Neither was very large. The oldest part of the city, Harmony, showed little evidence of planning: there were little narrow streets running at all angles, and the public squares were randomly placed. The northern part, Garrison, was smaller, but it had streets at precise right angles, and a big public plaza stood opposite the square fort at the northern edge.

All the buildings were low, with only a couple more than two stories high. The roofs were red tile, and the walls were whitewashed. Harmony reminded me of towns I'd seen in Mexico. Bright sun shone off the bay below the city bluff. Garrison was a harsher place, all right angles, neat and orderly, but every thing strictly functional. There was a square fortress at its northern edge. My new home.

I was a very junior lieutenant of CoDominium Marines, only three months out of the Academy and green as grass. It was Academy practice to commission the top thirty graduates in each class. The rest went out as cadets and midshipmen for more training. I was proud of the bars on my epaulets, but I was also a bit scared. I'd never been with troops before, and I'd never had any friends from the working classes, so I didn't know much about the kind of people who enlist in the Line Marines. I knew plenty of stories, of course. Men join to get away from their

wives, or because some judge gives them a chance to
enlist before passing sentence. Others are recruited
out of Bureau of Relocation ships. Most come from
Citizen classes, and my family's always been taxpayer.

It was just as well for me that my father was a
taxpayer. I grew up in the American Southwest,
where things haven't changed so much since the
CoDominium. We still think we're free men. When
my father died, Mom and I tried to run the ranch
the way he had, as if it still belonged to us. It did, on
paper, but we didn't have his contacts in the bureaucracy. We didn't understand all the regulations and
labor restrictions, and we didn't know who to bribe
when we broke the rules. When we got in real
trouble, I tried to keep the government people from
taking possession, and that wasn't too good an idea.
The judge was an old friend of my father's and offered to get me into the Academy. U.S. courts don't
have jurisdiction over CoDominium officers.

I didn't have a lot of choices, and CD Fleet service
looked pretty good just then. I'd not only get out of
trouble; I'd leave Earth. Mom was getting married
again, so she'd be all right. The government had the
ranch and we'd never get it back. I was young enough
to think soldiering was a romantic idea, and Judge
Hamilton made it pretty clear I was going to have to
do something.

"Look, Hal," he told me, "your dad should have
left. There's no place for people like us. They want
people who want security, who'll obey the rules—
people who *like* the welfare state, not ornery cusses
like you and your father. Even if I can get you off
this time, you'll get in trouble again. You're going to
have to leave, and you'll be better off as a CD officer
than as a colonist."

He was right. I wondered why he stayed. Same
reason my father did, I supposed. Getting older,

used to his home, not ready to go make a new start somewhere else. I hadn't said anything, but he must have guessed what I was thinking.

"I can still do some good here. I'm a judge for life—they can't take that away from me without damned good reasons—and I can still help kids like you. There's nothing here for you, Hal. The future's out there. New worlds, new ones found every year. Serve out a hitch in the Fleet service. See what's out there, and decide where you want your kids to grow up. Someplace free."

I couldn't think of anything else to do, so I let him get me into the Academy. It had been all right there. The Fleet has its own brotherhood. I'd been a loner most of my life, not because I wanted to be—God knows I would have liked to have friends!—but because I didn't fit in anywhere. The Academy was different. It's hard to say how. One thing, though, there aren't any incompetents whining to have the world take care of them. Not that we didn't look out for each other. If a classmate's soft on math, you help him, and if somebody has trouble with electronics—I did—a sharper classmate sits up nights boning up with him. But if after all that he can't cut it, he's out. There's more to it than that, though. I can't explain the Fleet's sense of brotherhood, but it's real enough, and it was what I'd been looking for all my life.

I was there two and a half years, and we worked all the time, cramming everything from weapons maintenance to basic science to civil engineering and road construction. I finished seventh in the class and got my commission. After a month's leave to say goodbye to my mother and my girl—only I didn't really have a girl; I just liked to pretend I did—I was on an Olympic Lines passenger ship headed for another star system.

And now I'm here, I thought. I looked down at the

planet, trying to spot places I'd seen on the maps in our briefing kit. I was also listening to the troopers in the compartment. The instructors at the Academy had told us that officers could learn a lot by listening to the men, and I hadn't had much opportunity to listen to these. Three weeks before I'd been on the passenger ship, and now I was at the end of nowhere on an ancient troop carrier, with a detachment commander who'd kept us training so hard there'd been no time for talk or anything else.

There were only a few viewports in the compartment, and those were taken by officers and senior enlisted men. Behind me, Sergeant Cernan was describing what he saw. A number of younger Marines, recruits mostly, were crowded around him. The older troopers were catching naps in their seats.

"Not much outside the city walls," Cernan said. "Trees, look like scrub oaks. And I think those others are olives. There's palms, too. Must be from Earth. Never saw palm trees that didn't come from Earth."

"Hey, Sarge, can you see the fort?" Corporal Roff asked.

"Yeah. Looks like any CD post. You'll be right at home."

"Sure we will," Roff said. "Sure. Christ, why us?"

"Your birthday present," Cernan said. "Just be damned glad you'll be leavin' someday. Think of them poor bastards back aft in the can."

The ship circled the harbor, then glided in on its stubby wings to settle into the chop outside the breakwater. The waves were two meters high and more, and the ship rolled badly. One of the new recruits was sick. His seatmate handed him a plastic bag.

"Hey, Dietz!" Roff called. "Want some fried bacon? A little salt pork?" He grinned. "Maybe some sow belly—"

"Sergeant Cernan."

"Sir!"

The captain didn't say anything else. He sat forward, a dozen rows in front of me, and I hadn't expected him to be listening, but I wasn't surprised. I'd learned in the past three weeks that not much went on without Captain John Christian Falkenberg finding out.

Behind me, Cernan said, very tight-lipped, "Roff, one more word out of you—"

Dietz's buddy found another bag. No one else kidded the sick recruits. Soon the shuttle moved into the inner harbor, where there were no waves, and everyone felt better. A lone tugboat came alongside and eased the spacecraft toward a concrete pier. There was no other traffic in the harbor except for a few small fishing boats.

A Navy officer came into the compartment and looked around until he found Falkenberg. "Sir, the Governor requests that you turn your men out under arms to assist in the prisoner formation."

Falkenberg turned toward the Navy man and raised an eyebrow. Then he nodded. "Sergeant Major!"

"Sir!" Ogilvie shouted from the rear of the compartment.

"Personal weapons for all troops. Rifles and cartridge belts. And bayonets, Sergeant Major. Bayonets, by all means."

"Sir." There was a bustle of activity as Sergeant Major Ogilvie and his weapons sergeants unlocked the arms chest and began passing out rifles.

"What about our other gear?" Falkenberg asked.

"You'll have to make arrangements with the garrison," the ship's officer said.

"Right. That's all, then?"

"Yes. That's all, Major."

I grinned as the Navyman left the compartment.

To the Navy there's only one captain aboard ship, and that's the skipper. Marine captains in transit get a very temporary and utterly meaningless "promotion" to major for the duration of the voyage.

Falkenberg went to the forward hatchway. "Lieutenant Slater. A moment, please."

"Sir." I went forward to join him. I hadn't really noticed the low gravity until I stood up, but now it was obvious. It was only eighty-five-percent Earth standard, and on the trip out, Falkenberg had insisted the Navy skipper keep the outer rim of the old troopship at one-hundred-ten-percent spin gravity for as much of the trip as possible. The Navy hadn't liked it, but they'd done it, and Falkenberg had trained us in the high-gravity areas. Now we felt as if we could float away with no trouble.

I didn't know much about Falkenberg. The Service List showed he'd had Navy experience, then transferred to Fleet Marines. Now he was with a Line outfit. Moving around like that, two transfers, should have meant he was being run out, but then there was his rank. He also had a Military Cross, but the List hadn't said what it was for. It did tell me he'd gone into the Academy at fifteen and left as a midshipman.

I first saw him at Betio Transfer Station, which is an airless rock the Fleet keeps as a repair base and supply depot. It's convenient to several important star systems, but there's nothing there. I'd been on my way from graduation to Crucis Sector Headquarters, with assignment to the Fleet Marines. I was proud of that. Of the three Marine branches, Fleet is supposed to be the technical elite. Garrison outfits are mostly for riot suppression. The Line Marines get the dirty jobs left over. Line troops say theirs is the real elite, and they certainly do more than their share of the actual fighting when things are tough. I didn't know if we'd be fighting on Arrarat. I didn't even know why we were sent here. I just knew that Falkenberg had authority to change orders for all unassigned officers, and I'd been yanked off my comfortable berth—first class, damn it!—to report to him at Betio. If he knew what was up, he wasn't telling the junior officers.

Falkenberg wasn't a lot older than I was. I was a few weeks past my twenty-first birthday, and he was maybe five years older, a captain with the Military Cross. He must have had something going for him— influence, possibly, but if that was it, why was he with the Line Marines and not on staff at headquarters? I couldn't ask him. He didn't talk very much. He wasn't unfriendly, but he seemed cold and distant and didn't encourage anyone to get close to him.

Falkenberg was tall, but he didn't reach my height, which is one hundred ninety-three centimeters according to my ID card. We called it six-four where I grew up. Falkenberg was maybe two inches shorter. His eyes were indeterminate in color, sometimes gray and sometimes green, depending on the light, and they seemed very bright when he looked at you. He had short hair the color of sand, and no moustache. Most officers grow them after they make captain, but he hadn't.

His uniforms always fit perfectly. I thought I cut a good military figure, but I found myself studying the way Falkenberg dressed. I also studied his mannerisms, wondering if I could copy any of them. I wasn't sure I liked him or that I really wanted to imitate him, but I told myself that anybody who could make captain before he was thirty was worth at least a bit of study. There are plenty of forty-year-old lieutenants in the service.

He didn't look big or particularly strong, but I knew better. I'm no forty-four-kilo weakling, but he threw me easily in unarmed combat practice, and that was in one-hundred-percent gravity.

He was grinning when I joined him at the forward hatchway. "Ever think, Lieutenant, that every military generation since World War One has thought theirs would be the last to carry bayonets?" He waved toward where Ogilvie was still passing out rifles.

"No, sir, I never did."

"Few do," Falkenberg said. "My old man was a CoDominium University professor, and he thought I ought to learn military history. Think about it: a weapon originally designed to convert a musket into a pike, and it's still around when we're going to war in starships."

"Yes, sir—"

"Because it's useful, Lieutenant—as you'll find out someday." The grin faded, and Falkenberg lowered his voice. "I didn't call you up here to discuss military history, of course. I want the men to see us in conference. Give them something to worry about. They know they're going ashore armed."

"Yes, sir—"

"Tell me, Harlan Slater, what do they call you?"

"Hal, sir." We had been aboard ship for twenty-one days, and this was the first time Falkenberg had asked. It says a lot about him.

"You're senior lieutenant," Falkenberg said.

"Yes, sir." Which wasn't saying much: the other lieutenants had all been classmates at the Academy, and I outranked them only because I'd graduated higher in the class.

"You'll collect the other officers and stay here at the gangway while we go through this prisoner formation. Then bring up the rear as we take the troops up the hill to the fort. I doubt there's transport, so we'll have to march."

"Yes, sir."

"You don't understand. If you don't understand something, ask about it. Have you noticed our troopers, Mr. Slater?"

"Frankly, Captain, I haven't had enough experience to make any kind of judgment," I said. "We have a lot of recruits—"

"Yes. I'm not worried about them. Nor about the regulars I brought with me to Betio. But for the rest, we've got the scrapings out of half the guardhouses in the Sector. I doubt they'll desert during their first hours ashore, but I'm going to make damned sure. Their gear will stay aboard this ship, and we'll march them up in formation. By dark I'll have turned this command over to Colonel Harrington and it will be his worry, but until then I'm responsible, and I'll see that every man gets to the fort."

"I see. Yes, sir." And that's why he's a captain at his age, on independent assignment at that. Efficient. I wanted to be like that, or thought I did. I wasn't quite sure what I really wanted. The CD Armed Services wasn't my idea, but now that I was in it, I wanted to do it right if I could. I had my doubts about some of the things the CoDominium did—I was glad that I hadn't been assigned to one of the regiments that puts down riots on Earth—but I didn't know what ought to replace the CD and the Grand Senate, either. After all, we did keep the peace, and that has to be worth a lot.

"They're opening the gangway," Falkenberg said. "Sergeant Major."

"Sir!"

"Column of fours in company order, please."

"Sir." Ogilvie began shouting orders. The troops marched down the gangway and onto the concrete pier below. I went out onto the gangway to watch.

It was hot outside and within minutes I was sweating. The sun seemed red-orange, and very bright.

After the smells of the troopship, with men confined with too little water for adequate washing, the planetary smells were a relief. Arrarat had a peculiar odor, slightly sweet, like flowers, with an undertone of wet vegetation. All that was mixed with the stronger smells of a salt sea and the harbor.

There were few buildings down at sea level. The city wall stood high above the harbor at the top of its bluff. Down on the level strip just above the sea were piers and warehouses, but the streets were wide and there were large spaces between buildings.

My first alien world. It didn't seem all that strange. I looked for something exotic, like sea creatures, or strange plants, but there weren't any visible from the gangway. I told myself all that would come later.

There was one larger structure at sea level. It was two stories high, with no windows facing us. It had big gates in the center of the wall facing the ship, with a guard tower at each of its corners. It looked like a prison, and I knew that was what it had to be, but there seemed no point in that. The whole planet was a prison.

There was a squad of local militiamen on the pier. They wore drab coveralls, which made quite a contrast to the blue and scarlet undress of the CoDominium Marines marching down the pier. Falkenberg talked with the locals for a moment, and then Sergeant Major Ogilvie shouted orders, and the Marines formed up in a double line that stretched up the dock to the aft gangway. The line went from the gangway to the big gates in the prison building. Ogilvie shouted more orders, and the Marines fixed bayonets.

They did it well. You'd never have known most of them were recruits. Even in the cramped quarters of the troop carrier, Falkenberg had drilled them into a smart-looking unit. The cost had been high. There were twenty-eight suicides among the recruits, and another hundred had been washed out and sent back among the convicts. They told us at the Academy that the only way to make a good Marine is to work him in training until he can have some pride in surviving it, and God knows Falkenberg must have believed that. It had seemed reasonable enough back in the lecture theater at Luna Base.

One morning we had four suicides, and one had been an old Line regular, not a recruit at all. I'd been duty officer when the troops found the body. It had been cut down from where he'd hanged himself to a light fixture, and the rope was missing. I tried to find the rope and even paraded all the men in that compartment, but nobody was saying anything.

Later Sergeant Major Ogilvie came to me in confidence. "You'll never find the rope, Lieutenant," he said. "It's cut up in a dozen pieces by now. That man had won the military medal. The rope he hanged himself with? That's lucky, sir. They'll keep the pieces."

All of which convinced me I had a lot to learn about Line Marines.

The forward companionway opened, and the convicts came out. Officially they were all convicts, or families of transportees who had voluntarily accompanied a convict; but when we'd gone recruiting in the prison section of the ship, we found a number of prisoners who'd never been convicted of anything at all. They'd been scooped up in one of Bureau of Relocation's periodic sweeps and put on the involuntary colonist list.

The prisoners were ragged and unwashed. Most wore BuRelock coveralls. Some carried pathetically small bundles, everything they owned. They milled around in confusion in the bright sunlight until ship's petty officers screamed at them and they shuffled down the gangway and along the pier. They tended to huddle together, shrinking away from the bayonets of the lines of troops on either side. Eventually they were herded through the big square gates of the prison building. I wondered what would happen to them in there.

There were more men than women, but there were plenty of women and girls. There were also far more children than I liked to see in that condition. I didn't like this. I hadn't joined the CoDominium Armed Services for this kind of duty.

"Heavy price, isn't it?" a voice said behind me. It was Deane Knowles. He'd been a classmate at the Academy. He was a short chap, not much above the minimum height for a commission, and had features so fine that he was almost pretty. I had reason to know that women liked him, and Deane liked them. He should have graduated second in the class, but he'd accumulated so many demerits for sneaking off bounds to see his girlfriends that he was dropped twenty-five places in class rank, which was why I outranked him and would until one of us was promoted above the other. I figured he'd make captain before I did.

"Heavy price for what?" I asked.

"For clean air and lower population and all the other goodies they have back on Earth. Sometimes I wonder if it's worth it."

"But what choices do we have?" I asked.

"None. Zero. Nothing else to do. Ship out the surplus and let 'em make their own way somewhere. In the long run it's not only all to the good, it's all there is; but the run doesn't look so long when you're watching the results. Look out. Here comes Louis."

Louis Bonneyman, another classmate, joined us. Louis had finished a genuine twenty-fourth in class rank. He was part French-Canadian, although he'd been raised in the U.S. most of his life. Louis was a fanatic CD loyalist and didn't like to hear any of us question CD policy, although, like the rest of us in the service, it didn't really matter what the policies were. "No politics in the Fleet" was beaten into our heads at the Academy, and later the instructors made it clear that what that really translated to was: "The Fleet is Our Fatherland." We could question anything the Grand Senate did—as long as we stood by our comrades and obeyed orders.

We stood there watching as the colonists were herded into the prison building. It took nearly an hour to get all two thousand of them inside. Finally the gates were closed. Ogilvie gave more orders and the Marines scabbarded their bayonets, then formed into a column of eight and marched down the road.

"Well, fellow musketeers," I said, "here we go. We're to follow up the hill, and there's apparently no transport."

"What about my ordnance?" Deane asked.

I shrugged. "Apparently arrangements will be made. In any event, it's John Christian Falkenberg's problem. Ours not to reason why—"

"Ours but to watch for deserters," Louis Bonneyman said. "And we'd best get at it. Is your sidearm loaded?"

"Oh, come on, Louis," Deane said.

"Notice," Louis said. "See how Falkenberg has formed up the troops. Recall that their baggage is still aboard. You may not like Falkenberg, Deane, but you will admit that he is thorough."

"As it happens, Louis is right," I said. "Falkenberg did say something about deserters. But he didn't think there'd be any."

"There you are," Louis said. "He takes no chances, that one."

"Except with us," Deane Knowles said.

"What do you mean by that?" Louis let the smile fade and lifted an eyebrow at Deane.

"Oh, nothing," Deane said. "Not much Falkenberg could do about it, anyway. But I don't suppose you chaps know what the local garrison commander asked for?"

"No, of course not," Louis said.

"How did you find out?" I asked.

"Simple. When you want to know something military, talk to the sergeants."

"Well?" Louis demanded.

Deane grinned. "Come on, we'll get too far behind. Looks as if we really will march all the way up the hill, doesn't it? Not even transport for officers. Shameful."

"Damn your eyes, Deane!" I said.

Knowles shrugged. "Well, the Governor asked for a full regiment and a destroyer. Instead of a regiment and a warship, he got us. Might be interesting if he really needed a regiment, eh? Coming, fellows?"

TWO

"I've a head like a concertina,
And I think I'm going to die,
And I'm here in the clink for a thunderin' drink,
And blackin' the corporal's eye. . . ."

"Picturesque," Louis said. "They sing well, don't they?"

"Shut up and walk," Deane told him. "It's bloody hot."

I didn't find it so bad. It was hot. No question about that, and undress blues were never designed for route marches on hot planets. Still, it could have been worse. We might have turned out in body armor.

There was no problem with the troops. They marched and sang like regulars, even if half of them were recruits and the rest were guardhouse cases. If any of them had ideas of running, they never showed them.

"With another man's cloak underneath of my head,
And a beautiful view of the yard,

It's thirty day's fine,
With bread and no wine,
For Drunk and Resistin' the Guard!
Mad-drunk and Resistin' the Guard!"

"Curious," Louis said. "Half of them have never seen a guardhouse."

"I expect they'll find out soon enough," Deane said. "Lord love us, will you look at that?"

He gestured at a row of cheap adobe houses along the riverbank. There wasn't much doubt about what they sold. The girls were dressed for hot weather, and they sat on the windowsills and waved at the troopers going by.

"I thought Arrarat was full of holy Joes," Louis Bonneyman said. "Well, we will have no difficulty finding any troopers who run—not for the first night, anyway."

The harbor area was just north of a wide river that fanned into a delta east of the city. The road was just inland from the harbor, with the city a high bluff to our right as we marched inland. It seemed a long way before we got to the turnoff to the city gate.

There were facilities for servicing the space shuttle, and some riverboat docks and warehouses, but it seemed to me there wasn't a lot of activity, and I wondered why. As far as I could remember, there weren't any railroads on Arrarat, nor many highways, and I couldn't remember seeing any airfields, either.

After a kilometer of marching inland, we turned sharply right and followed another road up the bluff. There was a rabbit warren of crumbling houses and alleys along the bluff, then a clear area in front of the high city wall. Militiamen in drab coveralls manned a guardhouse at the city gate. Other militiamen patrolled the wall. Inside the gate was Harmony, another warren of houses and shops not a lot different from those outside, but a little better kept up.

The main road had clear area for thirty meters on each side, and beyond that was chaos. Market stalls, houses, tailor shops, electronics shops, a smithy with hand bellows and forge, a shop that wound electric motors and another that sold solar cells, a pottery with kick-wheel where a woman shaped cups from clay, a silversmith, a scissors grinder—the variety was overwhelming, and so was the contrast of modern and the kinds of things you might see in Frontierland.

There were anachronisms everywhere, but I was used to them. The military services were shot through with contrasts. Part of it was the state of development out in the colonies—many of them had no industrial base, and some didn't want any to begin with. If you didn't bring it with you, you wouldn't have it. There was another reason, too. CoDominium Intelligence licensed all scientific research and tried to suppress anything that could have military value. The U.S.-Soviet alliance was on top and wasn't about to let any new discoveries upset the balance. They couldn't stop everything, but they didn't have to, so long as the Grand Senate controlled everyone's R&D budget and could tinker with the patent laws.

We all knew it couldn't last, but we didn't want to think about that. Back on Earth the U.S. and Soviet governments hated each other. The only thing they hated more was the idea that someone else—like the Chinese or Japanese or United Emirates—would get strong enough to tell them what to do. The Fleet guards an uneasy peace built on an uneasy alliance.

The people of Harmony came in all races and colors, and I heard a dozen languages shouted from shop to shop. Everyone either worked outside his house or had market stalls there. When we marched

past, people stopped work and waved at us. One old
man came out of a tailor shop and took off his broad-
brimmed hat. "God bless you, soldiers!" he shouted.
"We love you!"

"Now, that's what we joined up for," Deane said.
"Not to herd a bunch of losers halfway across the
Galaxy."

"Twenty parsecs isn't halfway across the Galaxy," I
told him.

He made faces at me.

"I wonder why they're all so glad to see us?" Louis
asked. "And they look hungry. How does one become so thin in an agricultural paradise?"

"Incredible," Deane said. "Louis, you really must
learn to pay attention to important details. Such as
reading the station roster of the garrison here."

"And when could I have done that?" Bonneyman
demanded. "Falkenberg had us working twelve hours
a day—"

"So you use the other twelve," Deane said.

"And what, O brilliant one, didst thou learn from
the station roster?" I asked.

"That the garrison commander is over seventy,
and he has one sixty-three-year-old major on his
staff, as well as a sixty-two-year-old captain. Also, the
youngest Marine officer on Arrarat is over sixty, and
the only junior officers are militia."

"Bah. A retirement post," Bonneyman said. "So
why did they ask for a regiment?"

"Don't be silly, Louis," Deane said. "Because
they've run into something they can't handle with
their militia and their superannuated officers, of
course."

"Meaning we'll have to," I said. Only, of course,
we didn't have a regiment, only less than a thousand
Marines, three junior officers, a captain with the
Military Cross, and—well, and nothing, unless the

local militia were capable of something. "The heroes have arrived."

"Yes. Nice, isn't it?" Deane said. "I expect the women will be friendly."

"And is that all you ever think about?" Louis demanded.

"What else is there? Marching in the sun?"

A younger townman in dark clerical clothing stood at his table under the awning of a sidewalk café. He raised a hand in a gesture of blessing. There were more cheers from a group of children.

"Nice to be loved," Deane said.

Despite the way he said it, Deane meant that. It was nice to be loved. I remembered my last visit to Earth. There were a lot of places where CD officers didn't dare go without a squad of troopers. Out here the people wanted us. The paladins, I thought, and I laughed at myself because I could imagine what Deane and Louis would say if I'd said that aloud, but I wondered if they didn't think it, too.

"They don't seem to have much transport," Louis said.

"Unless you count those." Deane pointed to a watering trough where five horses were tied. There were also two camels, and an animal that looked like a clumsy combination of camel, moose, and mule, with big splayed feet and silly antlers.

That had to be an alien beast, the first thing I was certain was native to this planet. I wondered what they called it, and how it had been domesticated.

There was almost no motor transport: a few pickup trucks, and one old ground-effects car with no top; everything else was animal transport. There were wagons, and men on horseback, and two women dressed in coveralls and mounted on mules.

Bonneyman shook his head. "Looks as if they stirred

up a brew from the American Wild West, medieval
Paris, and threw in scenes from the Arabian Nights."
	We all laughed, but Louis wasn't far wrong.

	Arrarat was discovered soon after the first private
exploration ships went out from Earth. It was an
inhabitable planet, and although there are a number
of those in the regions near Earth, they aren't all that
common. A survey team was sent to find out what
riches could be taken.
	There weren't any. Earth crops would grow, and
men could live on the planet, but no one was going
to invest money in agriculture. Shipping foodstuffs
through interstellar space is a simple way of going
bankrupt unless there are nearby markets with valuable minerals and no agriculture. This planet had no
nearby market at all.
	The American Express Company owned settlement
rights through discovery. AmEx sold the planet to a
combine of churches. The World Federation of
Churches named it Arrarat and advertised it as "a
place of refuge for the unwanted of Earth." They
began to raise money for its development, and since
this was before the Bureau of Relocation began involuntary colonies, they had a lot of help. Charity,
tithes, government grants, all helped, and then the
church groups hit on the idea of a lottery. Prizes
were free transportation to Arrarat for winners and
their families; and there were plenty of people willing to trade Earth for a place where there was free
land, plenty to eat, hard work, no government ha-
rassment, and no pollution. The World Federation of
Churches sold tens of millions of one-credit lottery
tickets. They soon had enough money to charter
ships and send people out.
	There was plenty of room for colonists, even though
the inhabitable portion of Arrarat is comparatively

small. The planet has a higher mean temperature than Earth, and the regions near the equator are far too hot for men to live in. At the very poles it is too cold. The southern hemisphere is nearly all water. Even so, there is plenty of land in the north temperate zone. The delta area where Harmony was founded was chosen as the best of the lot. It had a climate like the Mediterranean region of Earth. Rainfall was erratic, but the colony thrived.

The churches had very little money, but the planet didn't need heavy industry. Animals were shipped instead of tractors, on the theory that horses and oxen can make other horses and oxen, but tractors make only oil refineries and smog. Industry wasn't wanted; Arrarat was to be a place where each man could prune his own vineyard and sit in the shade of his fig tree. Some of the Federation of Churches' governing board actively hated industrial technology, and none loved it; and there was no need, anyway. The planet could easily support far more than the half to three-quarters of a million people the churches sent out as colonists.

Then the disaster struck. A survey ship found thorium and other valuable metals in the asteroid belt of Arrarat's system. It wasn't a disaster for everyone, of course. American Express was happy enough, and so was Kennicott Metals after they bought mining rights; but for the church groups it was disaster enough. The miners came, and with them came trouble. The only convenient place for the miners to go for recreation was Arrarat, and the kinds of establishments asteroid miners liked weren't what the Federation of Churches had in mind. The "Holy Joes" and the "Goddamns" shouted at each other and petitioned the Grand Senate for help, while the madams and gamblers and distillers set up for business.

That wasn't the worst of it. The Federation of

Churches' petition to the CoDominium Grand Senate ended up in the CD bureaucracy, and an official in Bureau of Corrections noticed that a lot of empty ships were going from Earth to Arrarat. They came back full of refined thorium, but they went out dead-head . . . and BuCorrect had plenty of prisoners they didn't know what to do with. It cost money to keep them. Why not, BuCorrect reasoned, send the prisoners to Arrarat and turn them loose? Earth would be free of them. It was humane. Better yet, the churches could hardly object to setting captives free. . . .

The BuCorrect official got a promotion, and Arrarat got over half a million criminals and convicts, most of whom had never lived outside a city. They knew nothing of farming, and they drifted to Harmony, where they tried to live as best they could. The result was predictable. Harmony soon had the highest crime rate in the history of man.

The situation was intolerable for Kennicott Metals. Miners wouldn't work without planet leave, but they didn't dare go to Harmony. Their union demanded that someone do something, and Kennicott appealed to the Grand Senate. A regiment of CoDominium Marines was sent to Arrarat. They couldn't stay long, but they didn't have to. They built walls around the city of Harmony, and for good measure they built the town of Garrison adjacent to it. Then the Marines put all the convicts outside the walls.

It wasn't intended to be a permanent solution. A CoDominium Governor was appointed, over the objections of the World Federation of Churches. The Colonial Bureau began preparations for sending a government team of judges and police and technicians and industrial-development specialists so that Arrarat could support the streams of people BuCorrect had sent. Before they arrived, Kennicott found an even more valuable source of thorium in a system nearer to Earth, the Arrarat mines were put into reserve, and there was no longer any reason for the CoDominium Grand Senate to be interested in Arrarat. The Marine garrison pulled out, leaving a cadre to help train colonial militia to defend the walls of Harmony-Garrison.

"What are you so moody about?" Deane asked.

"Just remembering what was in the briefing they gave us. You aren't the only one who studies up," I said.

"And what have you concluded?"

"Not a lot. I wonder how the people here like living in a prison. It's got to be that way, convicts outside and citizens inside. Marvelous."

"Perhaps they have a city jail," Louis said. "That would be a prison within a prison."

"Fun-ny," Deane said.

We walked along in silence, listening to the tramp of the boots ahead of us, until we came to another wall. There were guards at that gate, too. We passed through into the smaller city of Garrison.

"And why couldn't they have had transportation for officers?" Louis Bonneyman said. "There are trucks here."

There weren't many, but there were more than in Harmony. Most of the vehicles were surplus military ground-effects troop carriers. There were also more wagons.

"March or die, Louis. March or die." Deane grinned.

Louis said something under his breath. "March or Die" was a slogan of the old French Foreign Legion, and the Line Marines were direct descendants of the Legion, with a lot of their traditions. Bonneyman couldn't stand the idea that he wasn't living up to the service's standards.

Commands rattled down the ranks of marching men. "Look like Marines, damn you!" Ogilvie shouted.

"Falkenberg's showing off," Deane said.

"About time, too," Louis told him. "The fort is just ahead."

"Sound off!" Ogilvie ordered.

"We've left blood in the dirt of twenty-five worlds,
We've built roads on a dozen more,
And all that we have at the end of our hitch
Buys a night with a second-class whore.
The Senate decrees, the Grand Admiral calls,
The orders come down from on high.
It's 'On Full Kits' and 'Sound Board Ships,'
We're sending you where you can die."

Another Legion tradition, I thought. Over every orderly room door in Line regiments is a brass plaque. It says: YOU ARE LINE MARINES IN ORDER TO DIE, AND THE FLEET WILL SEND YOU WHERE YOU CAN DIE. An inheritance from La Légion Etrangère. The first time I saw it, I thought it was dashing and romantic, but now I wondered if they meant it.

The troops marched in the slow cadence of the Line Marines. It wasn't a fast pace, but we could keep it up long after quick-marching troops keeled over from exhaustion.

"The lands that we take, the Senate gives
    back,
Rather more often than not,
But the more that are killed, the less share the
    loot,
And we won't be back to this spot.

We'll break the hearts of your women and
    girls,
We may break your arse, as well,
Then the Line Marines with their banners
    unfurled
Will follow those banners to hell.
We know the devil, his pomps, and his works,
Ah, yes! We know them well!
When you've served out your hitch in the Line
    Marines,
You can bugger the Senate of Hell!"

"An opportunity we may all have," Deane said.
"Rather sooner than I'd like. What *do* they want with
us here?"
"I expect we'll find out soon enough," I said.

"Then we'll drink with our comrades and throw
    down our packs,
We'll rest ten years on the flat of our backs,
Then it's 'On Full Kits' and out of your racks,
You must build a new road through Hell!
The Fleet is our country, we sleep with a rifle,
No man ever begot a son on his rifle,
They pay us in gin and curse when we sin,
There's not one that can stand us unless we're
    downwind,
We're shot when we lose and turned out when
    we win,
But we bury our comrades wherever they fall,
And there's none that can face us, though we've
    nothing at all."

THREE

Officers' Row stretched along the east side of the parade ground. The fort was nothing special. It hadn't been built to withstand modern weapons, and it looked a bit like something out of *Beau Geste*, which was reasonable, since it was built of local materials by officers with no better engineering education than mine. It's simple enough to lay out a rectangular walled fort, and if that's enough for the job, why make it more complicated?

The officers' quarters seemed empty. The fort had been built to house a regimental combat team with plenty of support groups, and now there were fewer than a dozen Marine officers on the planet. Most of them lived in family quarters, and the militia officers generally lived in homes in the city. It left the rest of us with lots of room to rattle around in. Falkenberg drew a suite meant for the regimental adjutant, and I got a major's rooms myself.

After a work party brought our personal gear up from the landing boat, I got busy and unpacked, but when I finished, the place still looked empty. A

41

lieutenant's travel allowance isn't very large, and the rooms were too big. I stowed my gear and wondered what to do next. It seemed a depressing way to spend my first night on an alien world. Of course, I'd been to the Moon, and Mars, but those are different. They aren't worlds. You can't go outside, and you might as well be in a ship. I wondered if we'd be permitted off post—I was still thinking like a cadet, not an officer on field duty—and what I could do if we were. We'd had no instructions, and I decided I'd better wait for a briefing.

There was a quick knock on my door, and then it opened. An old Line private came in. He might have been my father. His uniform was tailored perfectly, but worn in places. There were hash marks from wrist to elbow.

"Private Hartz reporting, zur." He had a thick accent, but it wasn't pure anything; a lot of different accents blended together. "Sergeant Major sent me to be the lieutenant's dog-robber."

And what the hell do I do with him? I wondered. It wouldn't do to be indecisive. I couldn't remember if he'd been part of the detachment in the ship, or if he was one of the garrison. Falkenberg would never be in that situation. He'd know. The trooper was standing at attention in the doorway. "At ease, Hartz," I said. "What ought I to know about this place?"

"I don't know, zur."

Which meant he was a newcomer, or he wasn't spilling anything to officers, and I wasn't about to guess which. "Do you want a drink?"

"Thank you, yes, zur."

I found a bottle and put it out on the dressing stand. "Always leave two for me. Otherwise, help yourself," I told him.

He went to the latrine for glasses. I hadn't known there were any there, but then I wasn't all that familiar with senior officers' quarters. Maybe Hartz was, so I'd gained no information about him. He poured a shot for himself. "Is the lieutenant drinking?"

"Sure, I'll have one." I took the glass from him. "Cheers."

"*Prosit.*" He poured the whiskey down in one gulp. "I see the lieutenant has unpacked. I will straighten up now. By your leave, zur."

He wandered around the room, moving my spare boots two inches to the left, switching my combat armor from one side of the closet to the other, taking out my dress uniform and staring at it inch by inch.

I didn't need an orderly, but I couldn't just turn him out. I was supposed to get to know him, since he'd be with me on field duty. If any, I thought. To hell with it. "I'm going down to the officers' mess," I told him. "Help yourself to the bottle, but leave me two shots for tonight."

"Zur."

I felt like an idiot, chased out of my own quarters by my own batman, but I couldn't see what else to do. He was clearly not going to be satisfied until he'd gone over every piece of gear I had. Probably trying to impress me with how thorough he was. They pay dog-robbers extra, and it's always good duty for a drinking man. I was pretty sure I could trust him. I'd never crossed Ogilvie that I knew of. It takes a particularly stupid officer to get on the wrong side of the sergeant major.

It wasn't hard to find the officers' club. Like everything else, it had been built for a regiment, and it was a big building. I got a surprise inside. I was met by a Marine corporal I recognized as one of the detachment we'd brought with us. I started to go into the bar, where I saw a number of militia officers, and the corporal stopped me.

"Excuse me, sir. Marine club is that way." He pointed down the hall.

"I think I'd rather drink with the militiamen, Corporal."

"Yes, sir. Sergeant Major told me to be sure to tell all officers, sir."

"I see." I didn't see, but I wasn't going to get into an argument with a corporal, and there wasn't any point in being bullheaded. I went down the hall to the Marine club. Deane Knowles was already there. He was alone except for a waiter—another trooper from our detachment. In the militia bar the waiters were civilians.

"Welcome to the gay and merry life," Deane said. "Will you have whiskey? Or there's a peach brandy that's endurable. For God's sake, sit down and talk to me!"

"I take it you were intercepted by Corporal Hansner," I said.

"Quite efficiently. Now I know it is Fleet practice to carry the military caste system to extremes, but this seems a bit much, even so. There are, what, a dozen Marine officers here, even including our august selves. So we immediately form our own club."

I shrugged. "Maybe it's the militiamen who don't care for us?"

"Nonsense. Even if they hated our guts, they'd want news from Earth. Meanwhile, we find out nothing about the situation here. What's yours?"

"I'll try your brandy," I told the waiter. "And who's the bartender when you're not on duty?"

"Don't know, sir. Sergeant Major sent me over—"

"Yes, of course." I waited for the trooper to leave. "And Sergeant Major takes care of us, he does, indeed. I have a truly formidable orderly—"

Deane was laughing. "One of the ancients? Yes. I

thought so. As is mine. Monitor Armand Kubiak, at my service, sir."

"I only drew a private," I said.

"Well, at least Ogilvie has some sense of propriety," Deane said. "Cheers."

"Cheers. That's quite good, actually." I put the glass down and started to say something else, but Deane wasn't listening to me. He was staring at the door, and after a moment I turned to follow his gaze. "You know, I think that's the prettiest girl I ever saw."

"Certainly a contender," Deane said. "She's coming to our table."

"Obviously." We got to our feet.

She was definitely worth looking at. She wasn't very tall. Her head came about to my chin, so that with the slight heels on her sandals she was just taller than Deane. She wore a linen dress, blue to match her eyes, and it looked as if she'd never been out in the sun at all. The dress was crisp and looked cool. Few of the women we'd seen on the march in had worn skirts, and those had been long, drab cotton things. Her hair was curled into wisps around her shoulders. She had a big golden seal ring on her right hand.

She walked in as if she owned the place. She was obviously used to getting her own way.

"I hope you're looking for us," Deane said.

"As a matter of fact, I am." She had a very nice smile. An expensive smile, I decided.

"Well, you've excellent taste, anyway," Deane said.

I don't know how he gets away with it. I think it's telepathy. There's no particular cleverness to what he says to girls. I know, because I made a study of his technique when we were in the Academy. I thought I could learn it the way I was learning tactics, but it didn't work. What Deane says doesn't matter, and how he says it doesn't even seem important. He'll chatter along, saying nothing, even being offensive, and the next thing you know the girl's leaving with him. If she has to ditch a date, that can happen, too.

I was damned if it was going to happen this time, but I had a sinking feeling, because I'd been determined before and it hadn't done me any good. I couldn't think of one thing to say to her.

"I'm Deane Knowles. And this is Lieutenant Slater," Deane said.

You rotten swine, I thought. I tried to smile as she offered her hand.

"And I'm Irina Swale."

"Surely you're the Governor's daughter, then," Deane said.

"That's right. May I sit down?"

"Please do." Deane held her chair before I could get to it. It made me feel awkward. We managed to get seated, and Private Donnelley came over.

"Jericho, please," Irina said.

Donnelley looked blankly at her.

"He came in with us," I said. "He doesn't know what you've ordered."

"It's a wine," she said. "I'm sure there will be several bottles. It isn't usually chilled."

"Yes, ma'am," Donnelley said. He went over to the bar and began looking at bottles.

"We were just wondering what to do," Deane said. "You've rescued us from terminal ennui."

She smiled at that, but there was a shadow behind the smile. She didn't seem offended by us, but she wasn't really very amused. I wondered what she wanted.

Donnelley brought over a bottle and a wineglass. "Is this it, ma'am?"

"Yes. Thank you."

He put the glass on the table and poured. "If you'll excuse me a moment, Lieutenant Knowles?"

"Sure, Donnelley. Don't leave us alone too long, or we'll raid your bar."

"Yes, sir." Donnelley went out into the hall.

"Cheers," Deane said. "Tell us about the night life on Arrarat."

"It's not very pleasant," Irina said.

"Rather dull. Well, I guess we expected that—"

"It's not so much dull as horrible," Irina said. "I'm sorry. It's just that . . . I feel guilty when I think about my own problems. They're so petty. Tell me, when are the others coming?"

Deane and I exchanged glances. I started to say something, but Deane spoke first. "They don't tell us very much, you know."

"Then it's true—you are the only ones coming," she said.

"Now, I didn't say that," Deane protested. "I said I didn't know—"

"You needn't lie," she said. "I'm hardly a spy. You're all they sent, aren't you? No warship, and no regiment. Just a few hundred men and some junior officers."

"I'd have thought you'd know more than we do," I said.

"I just don't give up hope quite as quickly as my father does."

"I don't understand any of this," I said. "The Governor sent for a regiment, but nobody's told us what that regiment was supposed to do."

"Clean up the mess we've made of this planet," Irina said. "And I really thought they'd do something. The CoDominium has turned Arrarat into sheer hell, and I thought they'd have enough . . . what? Pride? Shame? Enough elementary decency to put things right before we pull out entirely. I see I was wrong."

"I take it things are pretty bad outside the walls," Deane said.

"Bad? They're horrible!" Irina said. "You can't even imagine what's happening out there. Criminal gangs setting themselves up as governments. And my father recognizes them as governments! We make treaties with them. And the colonists are ground to pieces. Murder's the least of it. A whole planet going to barbarism, and we don't even *try* to help them."

"But surely your militia can do something," Deane said.

"Not really." She shook her head, slowly, and stared into the empty wineglass. "In the first place, the militia won't go outside the walls. I don't suppose I blame them. They aren't soldiers. Shopkeepers, mostly. Once in a while they'll go as far as the big river bend, or down to the nearest farmlands, but that doesn't do any good. We tried doing something more permanent, but it didn't work. We couldn't protect the colonists from the convict gangs. And now we recognize convict gangsters as legal governments!"

Donnelley came back in and went to the bar. Deane signaled for refills.

"I noticed people came out to cheer us as we marched through the city," I said.

Irina's smile was bitter. "Yes. They think you're going to open up trade with the interior, rescue their relatives out there. I wish you could."

Before we could say anything else, Captain Falkenberg came in. "Good afternoon," he said. "May I join you?"

"Certainly, sir," Deane said. "This is Captain Falkenberg. Irina Swale, Captain, the Governor's daughter."

"I see. Good afternoon. Brandy, please, Donnelley. And will the rest of you join me? Excellent. Another round, please. Incidentally, my name is John. First names in the mess, Deane—except for the colonel."

"Yes, sir. Excuse me. John. Miss Swale has been telling us about conditions outside the walls. They're pretty bad."

"I gather. I've just spent the afternoon with the colonel. Perhaps we can do something, Miss Swale."

"Irina. First names in the mess." She laughed. It was a very nice laugh. "I wish you could do something for those people, but—well, you only have a thousand men."

"A thousand Line Marines," Falkenberg said. "That's not quite the same thing."

And we don't even have a thousand Marines, I told myself. Lot of recruits with us. I wondered what Falkenberg had in mind. Was he just trying to impress the Governor's daughter? I hoped not, because the way he'd said it made me feel proud.

"I gather you sympathize with the farmers out there," Falkenberg said.

"I'd have to, wouldn't I?" Irina said. "Even if they didn't come to me after Hugo—my father—says he can't help them. And I've tried to do something for the children. Do you really think—" She let her voice trail off.

Falkenberg shrugged. "Doubtless we'll try. We can put detachments out in some of the critical areas. As you said, there's only so much a thousand men can do, even a thousand Marines."

"And after you leave?" Irina said. Her voice was bitter. "They are pulling out, aren't they? You've come to evacuate us."

"The Grand Senate doesn't generally discuss high policy with junior captains," Falkenberg said.

"No, I suppose not. But I do know you brought

orders from the Colonial Office, and Hugo took them into his office to read them—and he hasn't spoken to anyone since. All day he's been in there. It isn't hard to guess what they say." Irina sipped at the wine and stared moodily at the oak table. "Of course it's necessary to understand the big picture. What's one little planet with fewer than a million people? Arrarat is no threat to the peace, is it? But they are people, and they deserve something better than— Sorry. I'm not always like this."

"We'll have to think of something to cheer you up," Deane said. "Tell me about the gay social life of Arrarat."

She gave a half smile. "Wild. One continuous whirl of grand balls and lewd parties. Just what you'd expect on a church-settled planet."

"Dullsville," Deane said. "But now that we're here—"

"I expect we can manage something," Irina said. "I tend to be Dad's social secretary. John, isn't it customary to welcome new troops with a formal party? We'll have to have one in the Governor's palace."

"It's customary," Falkenberg said. "But that's generally to welcome a regiment, not a random collection of replacements. On the other hand, since the replacements are the only military unit here—"

"Well, we do have our militia," Irina said.

"Sorry. I meant the only Line unit. I'm certain everyone would be pleased if you'd invite us to a formal ball. Can you arrange it for, say, five days from now?"

"Of course," she said. She looked at him curiously. So did the rest of us. It hadn't occurred to me that Falkenberg would be interested in something like that. "I'll have to get started right away, though."

"If that's cutting it too close," Falkenberg said, "we—"

"No, that will be all right."

Falkenberg glanced at his watch, then drained his glass. "One more round, gentlemen, and I fear I have to take you away. Staff briefing. Irina, will you need an escort?"

"No, of course not."

We chatted for a few minutes more, then Falkenberg stood. "Sorry to leave you alone, Irina, but we do have work to do."

"Yes. I quite understand."

"And I'll appreciate it if you can get that invitation made official as soon as possible," Falkenberg said. "Otherwise, we're likely to have conflicting duties, but, of course, we could hardly refuse the Governor's invitation."

"Yes, I'll get started right now," she said.

"Good. Gentlemen? We've a bit of work. Administration of the new troops and such. Dull, but necessary."

FOUR

The conference room had a long table large enough for a dozen officers, with chairs at the end for twice that many more. There were briefing screens on two walls. The others were paneled in some kind of rich wood native to Arrarat. There were scars on the paneling where pictures and banners had hung. Now the panels were bare, and the room looked empty and cold. The only decoration was the CoDominium flag, American eagle and Soviet hammer and sickle. It stood between an empty trophy case and a bare corner.

Louis Bonneyman was already there. He got up as we came in.

"There won't be many here," Falkenberg said. "You may as well take places near the head of the table."

"Will you be regimental adjutant or a battalion commander?" Deane asked me. He pointed to senior officers' places.

"Battalion commander, by all means," I said. "Line

over staff any day. Louis, you can be intelligence officer."

"That may not seem quite so amusing in a few minutes," Falkenberg said. "Take your places, gentlemen." He punched a button on the table's console. "And give some thought to what you say."

I wondered what the hell he meant by that. It hadn't escaped me that he'd known where to find us. Donnelley must have called him. The question was, why?

"Ten-hut!"

We got up as Colonel Harrington came in. Deane had told me Harrington was over seventy, but I hadn't really believed it. There wasn't any doubt about it now. Harrington was short and his face had a pinched look. The little hair he had left was white.

Sergeant Major Ogilvie came in with him. He looked enormous when he stood next to the Colonel. He was almost as tall as Falkenberg, anyway, and a lot more massive, a big man to begin with. Standing next to Harrington, he looked like a giant.

The third man was a major who couldn't have been much younger than the Colonel.

"Be seated, gentlemen," Harrington said. "Welcome to Arrarat. I'm Harrington, of course. This is Major Lorca, my Chief of Staff. We already know who you are."

We muttered some kind of response while Harrington took his seat. He sat carefully, the way you might in high gravity, only, of course, Arrarat isn't a high-gravity planet. Old, I thought. Old and past retirement, even with regeneration therapy and geriatric drugs.

"You're quite a problem for me," the Colonel said. "We asked for a regiment of military police. Garrison Marines. I didn't think we'd get a full regiment, but

I certainly didn't ask for Line troops. Now what am I to do with you?"

Nobody said anything.

"I cannot integrate Line Marines into the militia," the Colonel said. "It would be a disaster for both units. I don't even want your troops in this city! That's all I need, to have Line troopers practicing system D in Harmony!"

Deane looked blankly at me, and I grinned. It was nice to know something he didn't. System D is a Line troop tradition. The men organize themselves into small units and go into a section of town where they all drink until they can't hold any more. Then they tell the saloon owners they can't pay. If any of them causes trouble, they wreck his place, with the others converging onto the troublesome bar while more units delay the guard.

"I'm sorry, but I want your Line troopers out of this city as soon as possible," Harrington said. "And I can't give you any officers. There's no way I can put Marines under militia officers, and I can't spare any of the few Fleet people I have. That's a break for you, gentlemen, because the four of you will be the only officers in the 501st Provisional Battalion. Captain Falkenberg will command, of course. Mr. Slater, as senior lieutenant you will be his second, and I expect you'll have to take a company, as well. You others will also be company commanders. Major Lorca will be able to assist with logistics and maintenance services, but for the rest of it, you'll be on your own."

Harrington paused to let that sink in. Deane was grinning at me, and I answered it with one of my own. With any luck we'd do pretty well out of this miserable place. Experience as company commanders could cut years off our time as lieutenants.

"The next problem is, what the hell can I do with

you after you're organized?" Harrington demanded. "Major Lorca, if you'll give them the background?"

Lorca got up and went to the briefing stand. He used the console to project a city map on the briefing screen. "As you can see, the city is strongly defended," he said. "We have no difficulty in holding it with our militia. However, it is the only part of Arrarat that we have ever been required to hold, and as a result there are a number of competing gangs operating pretty well as they please in the interior. Lately a group calling itself the River Pack has taken a long stretch along the riverbanks and is levying such high passage fees that they have effectively cut this city off from supply. River traffic is the only feasible way to move agricultural goods from the farmlands to the city."

Lorca projected another map showing the river stretching northwestward from Harmony-Garrison. It ran through a line of hills; then upriver of that were more farmlands. Beyond them was another mountain chain. "In addition," Lorca said, "the raw materials for whatever industries we have on this planet come from these mines." A light pointer indicated the distant mountains. "It leaves us with a delicate political situation."

The Colonel growled like a dog. "Delicate. Hell, it's impossible!" he said. "Tell 'em the rest of it, Lorca."

"Yes, Colonel. The political responsibilities on this planet have never been carefully defined. Few jurisdictions are clear-cut. For example, the city of Garrison is under direct military authority, and Colonel Harrington is both civil and military commander within its walls. The city of Harmony is under direct CoDominium rule, with Governor Swale as its head. That is clear, but Governor Swale also holds a commission as planetary executive, which in theory subordinates Colonel Harrington to him. In practice they work together well enough, with the Governor taking civil authority and Colonel Harrington exercising military authority. In effect we have integrated Garrison and Harmony."

"And that's about all we've agreed on," Harrington said. "There's one other thing that's bloody clear. Our orders say we're to hold Garrison at all costs. That, in practice, means we have to defend Harmony as well, so we've an integrated militia force. There's plenty enough strength to defend both cities against direct attack. Supply's another matter."

"As I said, a delicate situation," Major Lorca said. "We cannot hold the city without supply, and we cannot supply the city without keeping the river transport lines open. In the past, Governor Swale and Colonel Harrington were agreed that the only way to do that was to extend CoDominium rule to these areas along the river." The light pointer moved again, indicating the area marked as held by the River Pack.

"They resisted us," Lorca said. "Not only the convicts, but the original colonists as well. Our convoys were attacked. Our militiamen were shot down by snipers. Bombs were thrown into the homes of militia officers—the hostiles don't have many sympathizers inside the city, but it doesn't take many to employ terror tactics. The Governor would not submit to military rule in the city of Harmony, and the militia could not sustain the effort needed to hold the riverbanks. On orders from the Governor, all CoDominium-controlled forces were withdrawn to within the walls of Harmony-Garrison."

"We abandoned those people," Harrington said. "Well, they got what they deserved. As you'd expect, there was a minor civil war out there. When it was over, the River Pack was in control. Swale recognized them as a legal government. Thought he could negotiate with them. Horse puckey. Go on, Lorca. Give 'em the bottom line."

"Yes, sir. As the Colonel said, the River Pack was recognized as a legal government, and negotiations were started. They have not been successful. The River Pack has made unacceptable demands as a condition of opening the river supply lines. Since it is obvious to the Governor that we cannot hold these cities without secure supplies, the Governor directed Colonel Harrington to re-open the supply lines by military force. The attempt was not successful."

"They beat our arses," Harrington said. His lips were tightly drawn. "I've got plenty of explanations for it. Militia are just the wrong kind of troops for the job. That's all burned hydrogen anyway. The fact is, they beat us, and we had to send back to Headquarters for Marine reinforcements. I asked for a destroyer and a regiment of military police. The warship and the Marines would have taken the goddam riverbanks, and the M.P.'s could hold it for us. Instead, I got you people."

"Which seems to have turned the trick," Major Lorca said. "At 1630 hours this afternoon, Governor Swale received word that the River Pack wishes to re-open negotiations. Apparently they have information sources within the city—"

"In the city, hell!" Harrington said. "In the Governor's palace, if you ask me. Some of his clerks have sold out."

"Yes, sir," Lorca said. "In any event, they have heard that reinforcements have come, and they wish to negotiate a settlement."

"Bastards," Colonel Harrington said. "Bloody criminal butchers. You can't imagine what those swine have done out there. And His Excellency will certainly negotiate a settlement that leaves them in control. I guess he has to. There's not much doubt that with the 501st as a spearhead we could retake that area, but we can't hold it with Line Marines! Hell, Line troops aren't any use as military government. They aren't trained for it and they won't do it."

Falkenberg cleared his throat. Harrington glared at him for a moment. "Yes?"

"Question, sir."

"Ask it."

"What would happen if the negotiations failed so that the 501st was required to clear the area by force? Would that produce a more desirable result?"

Harrington nodded, and the glare faded. "I like the way you think. Actually, Captain, it wouldn't, not really. The gangs would try to fight, but when they saw it was hopeless, they'd take their weapons and run. Melt into the bush and wait. Then we'd be back where we were a couple of years ago, fighting a long guerrilla war with no prospect for ending it. I had something like that in mind, Captain, but that was when I was expecting M.P.'s. I think we could govern with a regiment of M.P.'s."

"Yes, sir," Falkenberg said. "But even if we must negotiate a settlement with the River Pack, surely we would like to be in as strong a bargaining position as possible."

"What do you have in mind, Falkenberg?" Harrington asked. He sounded puzzled, but there was genuine interest in his voice.

"If I may, sir." Falkenberg got up and went to the briefing screen. "At the moment I take it we are technically in a state of war with the River Pack?"

"It's not that formal," Major Lorca said. "But, yes, that's about the situation."

"I noticed that there was an abandoned CD fort about two hundred forty kilometers upriver," Falkenberg said. He used the screen controls to show that section of the river. "You've said that you don't want Line Marines in the city. It seemed to me that the old fort would make a good base for the 501st, and our presence there would certainly help keep river traffic open."

"All right. Go on," Harrington said.

"Now we have not yet organized the 501st Battalion, but no one here knows that. I have carefully isolated my officers and troops from the militia. Sergeant Major, have any of the enlisted men talked with anyone on this post?"

"No, sir. Your orders were pretty clear, sir."

"And I know the officers have not," Falkenberg said. He glanced at us and we nodded. "Therefore, I think it highly unlikely that we will run into any serious opposition if we march immediately to our new base," Falkenberg said. "We may be able to do some good on the way. If we move fast, we may catch some River Pack gangsters. Whatever happens, we'll disrupt them and make it simpler to negotiate favorable terms."

"Immediately," Harrington said. "What do you mean by immediately?"

"Tonight, sir. Why not? The troops haven't got settled in. They're prepared to march. Our gear is all packed for travel. If Major Lorca can supply us with a few trucks for heavy equipment, we'll have no other difficulties."

"By God," Harrington said. He looked thoughtful. "It's taking a hell of a risk—" He looked thoughtful again. "But not so big a risk as we'd have if you stayed around here. As you say. Right now nobody knows what we've got. Let the troops get to talking, and it'll get all over this planet that you've brought a random collection of recruits, guardhouse soldiers, and newlies. That wouldn't be so obvious if you hit the road."

"You'd be pretty much on your own until we get the river traffic established again," Major Lorca said.

"Yes, sir," Falkenberg answered. "But we'd be closer to food supply than you are. I've got three helicopters and a couple of Skyhooks. We can bring in military stores with those."

"By God, I like it," Harrington said. "Right now those bastards have beaten us. I wouldn't mind paying them out." He looked at us, then shook his head. "What do you chaps think? I can spare only the four of you. That stands. Can you do it?"

We all nodded. I had my doubts, but I was cocky enough to think I could do anything. "It will be a cakewalk, sir," I said. "I can't think a gang of criminals wants to face a battalion of Line Marines."

"Honor of the corps and all that," Harrington said. "I was never with Line troops. You haven't been with 'em long enough to know anything about them, and here you're talking like one of them already. All right. Captain Falkenberg, you are authorized to take your battalion to Fort Beersheba at your earliest convenience. Tell 'em what you can give 'em, Lorca." The Colonel sounded ten years younger. That defeat had hurt him, and he was looking forward to showing the River Pack what regular troops could do.

Major Lorca told us about logistics and transport. There weren't enough trucks to carry more than a bare minimum of supplies. We could tow the artillery, and there were two tanks we could have. For most of us it would be march or die, but it didn't look to me as if there'd be very much dying.

Finally Lorca finished. "Questions?" he said. He looked at Falkenberg.

"I'll reserve mine for the moment, sir." Falkenberg was already talking like a battalion commander.

"Sir, why is there so little motor transport?" Louis Bonneyman asked.

"No fuel facilities," Lorca told him. "No petroleum refineries. We have a small supply of crude oil and a couple of very primitive distillation plants, but nowhere near enough to support any large number of motor vehicles. The original colonists were quite happy about that. They didn't want them." Lorca reminded me of one of the instructor officers at the Academy.

"What weapons are we facing?" Deane Knowles asked.

Lorca shrugged. "They're better armed than you think. Good rifles. Some rocket launchers. A few mortars. Nothing heavy, and they tend to be deficient in communications, in electronics in general, but there are exceptions to that. They've captured gear from our militia"—Colonel Harrington winced at that—"and, of course, anything we sell to the farmers eventually ends up in the hands of the gangs. If we refuse to let the farmers buy weapons, we condemn them. If we do sell weapons, we arm more convicts. A vicious circle."

I studied the map problem. It didn't look difficult. A thousand men need just over a metric ton of dried food every day. There was plenty of water along the route, though, and we could probably get local forage, as well. We could do it, even with the inadequate transport Lorca could give us. It did look like a cakewalk.

I worried with the figures until I was satisfied, then suddenly realized it wasn't an exercise for a class. This was real. In a few hours we'd be marching into hostile territory. I looked over at my classmates. Deane was punching numbers into his pocket computer and frowning at the result. Louis Bonneyman was grinning like a thief. He caught my eye and winked. I grinned back at him, and it made me feel better. Whatever happened, I could count on them.

Lorca went through a few more details on stores and equipment available from the garrison, plus other logistic support available from the fort. We all took notes, and of course the briefing was recorded. "That about sums it up," he said.

Harrington stood, and we got up. "I expect you'll want to organize the 501st before you'll have any meaningful questions," Harrington said. "I'll leave you to that. You may consider this meeting your formal call on the commanding officer, although I'll be glad to see any of you in my office if you've anything to say to me. That's all."

"Ten-hut!" Ogilvie said. He stayed in the briefing room as Colonel Harrington and Major Lorca left.

"Well. We've work to do," Falkenberg said. "Sergeant Major."

"Sir!"

"Please run through the organization we worked out."

"Sir!" Ogilvie used the screen controls to flash charts onto the screens. As the Colonel had said, I was second in command of the battalion, and also A Company commander. My company was a rifle outfit. I noticed it was heavy with experienced Line troopers, and I had less than my share of recruits.

Deane had drawn the weapons company, which figured. Deane had taken top marks in weapons technology at the Academy, and he was always reading up on artillery tactics. Louis Bonneyman had another rifle company with a heavy proportion of recruits to worry about. Falkenberg had kept a large headquarters platoon under his personal command.

"There are reasons for this structure," Falkenberg said. "I'll explain them later. For the moment, have any of you objections?"

"Don't know enough to object, sir," I said. I was studying the organization chart.

"All of you will have to rely heavily on your NCO's," Falkenberg said. "Fortunately, there are some good ones. I've given the best, Centurion Lieberman, to A Company. Bonneyman gets Sergeant Cernan. If he works out, we can get him a Centurion's badges. Knowles has already worked with Gunner-Centurion Pniff. Sergeant Major Ogilvie stays with Headquarters Platoon, of course. In addition to your command duties, each of you will have to fill some staff slots. Bonneyman will be intelligence." Falkenberg grinned slightly. "I told you it might not seem such a joke."

Louis answered his grin. He was already sitting in the regimental intelligence officer's chair at the table. I wondered why Falkenberg had given that job to Louis. Of the four of us, Louis had paid the least attention to his briefing packet, and he didn't seem cut out for the job.

"Supply and logistics stay with Knowles, of course," Falkenberg said. "I'll keep training myself. Now, I have a proposition for you. The Colonel has ordered us to occupy Fort Beersheba at the earliest feasible moment. If we simply march there with no fighting and without accomplishing much beyond getting there, the Governor will negotiate a peace. We will be stationed out in the middle of nowhere, with few duties beyond patrols. Does anyone see any problems with that?"

"Damned dull," Louis Bonneyman said.

"And not just for us. What have you to say, Sergeant Major?"

Ogilvie shook his head. "Don't like it, sir. Might be all right for the recruits, but wouldn't recommend it for the old hands. Especially the ones you took out of the brig. Be a lot of the bug, sir."

The bug. The Foreign Legion called it *le cafard*, which means the same thing. It had been the biggest single cause of death in the Legion, and it was still that among Line Marines. Men with nothing to do. Armed men, warriors, bored stiff. They get obsessed with the bug until they commit suicide, or murder, or desert, or plot mutiny. The textbook remedy for *le cafard* is a rifle and plenty of chances to use it. Combat. Line troops on garrison duty lose more men to *cafard* than active outfits lose in combat. So my instructors had told us, anyway.

"It will be doubly bad in this case," Falkenberg said. "No regimental pride. No accomplishments to brag about. No battles. I'd like to avoid that."

"How, sir?" Bonneyman asked.

Falkenberg seemed to ignore him. He adjusted the map until the section between the city and Fort Beersheba filled the screen. "We march up the Jordan," he said. "I suppose it was inevitable that the Federation of Churches would call the planet's most important river 'Jordan,' wasn't it? We march northwest, and what happens, Mr. Slater?"

I thought about it. "They run, I suppose. I can't think they'll want to fight. We've much better equipment than they have."

"Equipment and men," Falkenberg said. "And a damned frightening reputation. They already know we've landed, and they've asked for negotiatons. They've got sources inside the palace. You heard me arrange for a social invitation for five days from now."

We all laughed. Falkenberg nodded. "Which means that if we march tonight, we'll achieve *real* surprise. We can catch a number of them unaware and disarm them. What I'd like to do, though, is disarm the lot of them."

I was studying the map, and I thought I saw what he meant. "They'll just about have to retreat right past Fort Beersheba," I said. "Everything narrows down there."

"Precisely," Falkenberg said. "If we held the fort,

we could disarm everyone coming through. Furthermore, it is our fort, and we've orders to occupy it quickly. I remind you also that we're technically at war with the River Pack."

"Yes, but how do we get there?" I asked. "Also, Captain, if we're holding the bottleneck, the rest of them will fight. They can't retreat."

"Not without losing their weapons," Falkenberg said. "I don't think the Colonel would be unhappy if we *really* pacified that area. Nor do I think the militia would have all that much trouble holding it if we defeated the River Pack and disarmed their survivors."

"But as Hal asked, how do we get there?" Louis demanded.

Falkenberg said, "I mentioned helicopters. Sergeant Major has found enough fuel to keep them flying for a while."

"Sir, I believe there was something in the briefing kit about losses from the militia arsenal," Deane said. "Specifically including Skyhawk missiles. Choppers wouldn't stand a chance against those."

"Not if anyone with a Skyhawk knew they were coming," Falkenberg agreed. "But why should they expect us? The gear's at the landing dock. Nothing suspicious about a work party going down there tonight. Nothing suspicious about getting the choppers set up and working. I can't believe they expect us to take Beersheba tonight, not when they've every reason to believe we'll be attending a grand ball in five days."

"Yes, sir," Deane agreed. "But we can't put enough equipment into three choppers! The men who take Beersheba will be doomed. Nobody can march up that road fast enough to relieve them."

Falkenberg's voice was conversational. He looked up at the ceiling. "I did mention Skyhooks, didn't I?

Two of them. Lifting capacity in this gravity and atmosphere, six metric tons each. That's forty-five men with full rations and ammunition. Gentlemen, by dawn we could have ninety combat Marines in position at Fort Beersheba, with the rest of the 501st marching to their relief. Are you game?"

FIVE

It was cold down by the docks. A chill wind had blown in just after sundown, and despite the previous heat of the day I was shivering. Maybe, I thought, it isn't the cold.

The night sky was clear, with what seemed like millions of stars. I could recognize most of the constellations, and that seemed strange. It reminded me that although we were so far from Earth that a man who began walking in the time of the dinosaurs wouldn't have gotten here yet, it was still an insignificant distance to the universe. That made me feel small, and I didn't like it.

The troops were turned out in work fatigues. Our combat clothing and armor were still tucked away in the packs we were loading onto the Skyhook platforms. We worked under bright lights, and anyone watching would never have known we were anything but a work party. Falkenberg was sure that at least one pair of night glasses was trained on us from the bluff above.

The Skyhook platforms were light aluminum affairs, just a flat plate eight meters on a side with a meter-high railing around the perimeter. We stowed packs onto them. We also piled on other objects: light machine guns recoilless cannon, mortars, and boxes of shells and grenades. Some of the boxes had false labels on them, stenciled on by troops working inside the warehouse, so that watchers would see what looked like office supplies and spare clothing going aboard.

A truck came down from the fort and went into the warehouse. It seemed to be empty, but it carried rifles for ninety men. The rifles went into bags and were stowed on the Skyhooks.

Arrarat has only one moon, smaller than Earth's and closer. It was a bloody crescent sinking into the highlands to the west, and it didn't give much light. It would be gone in an hour. I wandered over to where Deane was supervising the work on the helicopters.

"Sure you have those things put together right?" I asked him.

"Nothing to it."

"Yeah. I hope not. It's going to be hard to find those landing areas."

"You'll be all right." He wasn't really listening to me. He had two communications specialists working on the navigation computers, and he kept glaring at the squiggles on their scopes. "That's good," he said. "Now feed in the test problem."

When I left to go find Falkenberg, Deane didn't notice I'd gone. Captain Falkenberg was inside the warehouse. "We've about got the gear loaded, sir," I told him.

"Good. Come have some coffee." One of the mess sergeants had set up the makings for coffee in one corner of the big high-bay building. There was also a map table, and Sergeant Major Ogilvie had a communications center set up there. Falkenberg poured two cups of coffee and handed one to me. "Nervous?" he asked me.

"Some."

"You can still call it off. No discredit. I'll tell the others there were technical problems. We'll still march in the morning."

"I'll be all right, sir."

He looked at me over the lip of his coffee cup. "I expect you will be. I don't like sending you into this, but there's no other way we can do it."

"Yes, sir," I said.

"You'll be all right. You've got steady troopers."

"Yes, sir." I didn't know any of the men, of course. They were only names and service records, not even that, just a statistical summary of service records, a tape spewed out by the personnel computer. Thirty had been let out of the brig for voluntary service in Arrarat. Another twenty were recruits. The rest were Line Marines, long service volunteers.

Falkenberg used the controls to project a map of the area around Beersheba onto the map table. "Expect you've got this memorized," he said.

"Pretty well, sir."

He leaned over the table and looked at the fort, then at the line of hills north of it. "You've some margin for error, I think. I'll have to leave to you the final decision on using the chopper in the actual assault. You can risk one helicopter. Not both. I must have one helicopter back, even if that costs you the mission. Is that understood?"

"Yes, sir." I could feel a sharp ball in my guts, and I didn't like it. I hoped it wouldn't show.

"Getting on for time," Falkenberg said. "You'll need all the time you can get. We could wait a day to get better prepared, but I think surprise is your best edge."

I nodded. We'd been through all this before. Was he talking because he was nervous, too? Or to keep me talking so I wouldn't brood?

"You may get a commendation out of this."

"If it's all the same to you, I'd rather have a guarantee that you'll show up on time." I grinned when I said it, to show I didn't mean it, but I did. Why the hell wasn't he leading this assault? The whole damned idea was his, and so was the battle plan. It was his show, and he wasn't going. I didn't want to think about the reasons. I had to depend on him to bail me out, and I couldn't even let myself think the word "coward."

"Time to load up," Falkenberg said.

I nodded and drained the coffee cup. It tasted good. I wondered if that would be the last coffee I'd ever drink. It was certain that some of us wouldn't be coming back.

Falkenberg clapped his hand on my shoulder. "You'll give them a hell of a shock, Hal. Let's get on with it."

"Right." But I sure wish you were coming with me.

I found Centurion Lieberman. We'd spent several hours together since Falkenberg's briefing, and I was sure I could trust him. Lieberman was about Falkenberg's height, built somewhere between wiry and skinny. He was about forty-five, and there were scars on his neck. The scars ran down under his tunic. He'd had a lot of regeneration therapy in his time.

His campaign ribbons made two neat rows on his undress blues. From his folder I knew he was entitled to another row he didn't bother to wear.

"Load 'em up," I told him.

"Sir." He spoke in a quiet voice, but it carried through the warehouse. "First and second platoons A Company, take positions on the Skyhook platforms."

The men piled in on top of the gear. It was crowded on the platforms. I got in with one group, and Lieberman boarded the other platform. I'd rather have been up in the helicopter, flying it or sitting next to the pilot, but I thought I was needed down here. Louis Bonneyman was flying my chopper. Sergeant Doty of Headquarters Platoon had the other.

"Bags in position," Gunner-Centurion Pniff said. "Stand ready to inflate Number One." He walked around the platform looking critically at the lines that led from it to the amorphous shape that lay next to it. "Looks good. Inflate Number One."

There was a loud hiss, and a great ghostly bag formed. It began to rise until it was above my platform. The plastic gleamed in the artificial light streaming from inside the warehouse. The bag billowed up until it was huge above us, and still it grew as the compressed helium poured out of the inflating cylinders. It looked bigger than the warehouse before Pniff was satisfied. "Good," he said. "Belay! Stand by to inflate Number Two."

"Jeez," one of the recruits said. "We going up in this balloon? Christ, we don't have parachutes! We can't go up in a balloon!"

Some of the others began to chatter. "Sergeant Ardwain," I said.

"Sir!"

I didn't say anything else. Ardwain cursed and crawled over to the recruits. "No chutes means we don't have to jump," he said. "Now shut up."

Number Two Skyhook was growing huge. It looked even larger than our own, because I could see all of it, and all I could see of the bag above us was this bloated thing filling the sky above me. The choppers started up, and after a moment they lifted. One rose directly above us. The other went to hover above the other Skyhook. The chopper looked dwarfed next to that huge bag.

The choppers settled onto the bags. Up on top the helicopter crews were floundering around on the billowing stuff to make certain the fastenings were set right. I could hear their reports in my helmet phones. Finally they had it all right.

"Everything ready aboard?" Falkenberg asked me. His voice was unemotional in the phones. I could see him standing by the warehouse doors, and I waved. "All correct, sir," I said.

"Good. Send Number One along, Gunner."

"Sir!" Pniff said. "Ground crews stand by. Let go Number One."

The troops outside were grinning at us as they cut loose the tethers holding the balloons. Nothing happened, of course; the idea of Skyhook is to have almost neutral buoyancy, so that the lift from the gas bags just balances the weight of the load. The helicopters provide all the motive power.

The chopper engines rose in pitch, and we lifted off. A gust of wind caught us and we swayed badly as we lifted. Some of the troops cursed, and their noncoms glared at them. Then we were above the harbor, rising to the level of the city bluff, then higher than that. We moved northward toward the fort, staying high above the city until we got to Garrison's north edge, then dipping low at the fortress wall.

Anyone watching from the harbor area would think we'd just ferried a lot of supplies up onto the bluff. They might wonder about carrying men as well, but we could be pretty sure they wouldn't suspect we were doing anything but ferrying them.

We dropped low over the fields north of the city and continued moving. Then we rose again, getting higher and higher until we were at thirty-three hundred meters.

The men looked at me nervously. They watched the city lights dwindle behind us.

"All right," I said. It was strange how quiet it was. The choppers were ultra-quiet, and what little noise they made was shielded by the gas bag above us. The railings cut off most of the wind. "I want every man to get his combat helmet on."

There was some confused rooting around as the men found their own packs and got their helmets swapped around. We'd been cautioned not to shift weight on the platforms, and nobody wanted to make any sudden moves.

I switched my command set to lowest power so it couldn't be intercepted more than a kilometer away. We were over three klicks high, so I wasn't much worried that anyone was listening. "By now you've figured that we aren't going straight back to the fort," I said.

There were laughs from the recruits. The older hands looked bored.

"We've got a combat mission," I said. "We're going two hundred fifty klicks west of the city. When we get there, we take a former CD fort, dig in, and wait for the rest of the battalion to march out and bring us home."

A couple of troopers perked up at that. I heard one tell his buddy, "Sure beats hell out of marching two hundred fifty klicks."

"You'll get to march, though," I said. "The plan is to land about eight klicks from the fort and march overland to take it by surprise. I doubt anyone is expecting us."

"Christ Johnny strikes again," someone muttered. I couldn't see who had said that.

"Sir?" a corporal asked. I recognized him: Roff, the man who'd been riding the seasick recruit in the landing boat.

"Yes, Corporal Roff?"

"Question, sir."

"Ask it."

"How long will we be there, Lieutenant?"

"Until Captain Falkenberg comes for us," I said.

"Aye, aye, sir."

There weren't any other questions. I thought that was strange. They must want to know more. Some of you will get killed tonight, I thought. Why don't you want to know more about it?

They were more interested in the balloon. Now that it didn't look as if it would fall, they wanted to look out over the edge. I had the non-coms rotate the men so everyone got a chance.

I'd had my look over the edge, and I didn't like it. Below the level of the railing it wasn't so bad, but looking down was horrible. Besides, there wasn't really anything to see, except a few lights, way down below, and far behind us a dark shape that sometimes blotted out stars: Number Two, about a klick away.

"Would the lieutenant care for coffee?" a voice asked me. "I have brought the flask."

I looked up to see Hartz with my Thermos and a mess-hall cup. I'd seen him get aboard with his communications gear, but I'd forgotten him after that. "Thanks, I'll have some," I said.

It was about half brandy. I nearly choked. Hartz didn't even crack a smile.

We took a roundabout way so that we wouldn't pass over any of the river encampments. The way led far north of the river, then angled southwest to our landing zone. I turned to look over the edge again, and I hoped that Deane had gotten the navigation computers tuned up properly, because there wasn't anything to navigate by down there. Once in a while there was an orange-yellow light, probably a farm-house, possibly an outlaw encampment, but otherwise all the hills looked the same.

This has got to be the dumbest stunt in military history, I told myself, but I didn't really believe it. The Line Marines had a long reputation for going into battle in newly formed outfits with strange officers. Even so, I doubted if any expedition had ever had so little going for it: a newlie commander, men who'd never served together, and a captain who'd plan the mission but wouldn't go on it. I told myself the time to object had been back in the briefing. It was a bit late now.

I looked at my watch. Another hour of flying time. "Sergeant Ardwain."

"Sir?"

"Get them out of those work clothes and into combat leathers and armor. Weapons check after everyone's dressed." Dressed to kill, I thought, but I didn't say it. It was an old joke, never funny to begin with. I wondered who thought of it first. Possibly some trooper outside the walls of Troy.

Hartz already had my leathers out of my pack. He helped me squirm out of my undress blues and into the synthi-leather tunic and trousers. The platform rocked as men tried to pull on their pants without standing up. It was hard to dress because we were sprawled out on our packs and other equipment. There was a lot of cursing as troopers moved around to find their own packs and rifles.

"Get your goddam foot out of my eye!"

"Shut up, Traeger."

Finally everyone had his armor on and his fatigues packed away. The troopers sat quietly now. Even the old hands weren't joking. There's something about combat armor that makes everything seem real.

They looked dangerous in their bulky leathers and

armor, and they were. The armor alone gave us a big edge on anything we'd meet here. It also gives a feeling of safety, and that can be dangerous. Nemourlon will stop most fragments and even pistol bullets, but it won't stop a high-velocity rifle slug.

"How you doing down there?" Louis's voice in my phones startled me for a moment.

"We're all armored up," I told him. "You still think you know where you're going?"

"Nope. But the computer does. Got a radar check five minutes ago. Forking stream that shows on the map. We're right on the button."

"What's our ETA?" I asked.

"About twenty minutes. Wind's nice and steady, not too strong. Piece of cake."

"Fuel supply?" I asked.

"We're hip-deep in spare cans. Not exactly a surplus, but there's enough. Quit worrying."

"Yeah."

"You know," Louis said, "I never flew a chopper with one of those things hanging off it."

"Now you tell me."

"Nothing to it," Louis said. "Handles a bit funny, but I got used to it."

"You'd better have."

"Just leave the driving to us. Out."

The next twenty minutes seemed like a week. I guarantee one way to stretch time is to sit on an open platform at thirty-three hundred meters and watch the night sky while you wait to command your first combat mission. I tried to think of something cheerful to say, but I couldn't, and I thought it was better just to be quiet. The more I talked, the more chance I'd show some kind of strain in my voice.

"Your job is to look confident," Falkenberg had told me. I hoped I was doing that.

*   *   *

"Okay, you can get your first look now," Louis said.

"Rojj." I got my night glasses from Hartz. They were better than issue equipment, a pair of ten-cm Leica light-amplifying glasses I bought myself when I left the Academy. A lot of officers do, because Leica makes a special offer for graduating cadets. I clipped them onto my helmet and scanned the hillside. The landing zone was the top of a peak which was the highest point on a ridge leading from the river. I turned the glasses to full power and examined the area carefully.

It looked deserted. There was some kind of scrubby chaparral growing all over it, and it didn't look as if anybody had ever been to the peak.

"Looks good to me," I told Louis. "What do you have?"

"Nothing on IR, nothing on low-light TV," he said. "Nothing barring a few small animals and some birds roosting in the trees. I like that. If there're animals and birds, there's probably no people."

"Yeah—"

"Okay, that's passive sensors. Should I take a sweep with K-band?"

I thought about it. If there were anyone down there, and that theoretical someone had a radar receiver, the chopper would give itself away with the first pulse. Maybe that would be better. "Yes."

"Rojj," Louis said. He was silent a moment. "Hal, I get nothing. If there's anybody down there, he's dug in good and expecting us."

"Let's go in," I said.

And now, I thought, I'm committed.

SIX

"Over the side!" Ardwain shouted. "Get those tethers planted! First squad take perimeter guard! Move, damn you!"

The men scrambled off the platform. Some of them had tether stakes, big aluminum corkscrews, which they planted in the ground. Others lashed the platform to the stakes. The first squad, two maniples, fanned out around the area with their rifles ready.

There wasn't much wind, but that big gas bag had a lot of surface area, and I was worried about it. I got off and moved away to look at it. It didn't seem to be too much strain on the tether stakes. The hillside was quiet and dark. We'd set down on top of some low bushes with stiff branches. The leaves felt greasy when they were crushed. I listened, then turned my surveillance amplifier to high gain. Still nothing, not even a bird. Nothing but my own troops moving about. I switched to general command frequency. "Freeze," I said.

The noise stopped. There was silence except for

the low "whump!" of the chopper blades, and a fainter sound from Number Two out there somewhere.

"Carry on," I said.

Ardwain came up to me. "Nobody here, sir. Area secure."

"Thank you." I thumbed my command set onto the chopper's frequency. "You can cut yourself loose, and bring in Number Two."

"Aye, aye, sir," Louis said.

We began pulling gear off the platform. After a few moments, Number Two chopper came in. We couldn't see the helicopter at all, only the huge gas bag with its platform dangling below it. The Skyhook settled onto the chaparral and men bailed out with tether stakes. Centurion Lieberman watched until he was sure the platform was secure, then ran over to me.

"All's well?" I asked him.

"Yes, sir." His tone made it obvious he'd wanted to say "of course."

"Get 'em saddled up," I said. "We're moving out."

"Aye, aye, sir. I still think Ardwain would be all right here, sir."

"No. I'll want an experienced man in case something happens. If we don't send for the heavy equipment, or if something happens to me, call Falkenberg for instructions."

"Aye, aye, sir." He still didn't like it. He wanted to come with us. For that matter, I wanted him along, but I had to leave a crew with the Skyhooks and choppers. If the wind came up so tethers wouldn't hold, those things had to get airborne fast, and the rest of us would be without packs and supplies. There were all kinds of contingencies, and I wanted a reliable man I could trust to deal with them.

"We're ready, sir," Ardwain said.

"Right. Let's move out." I switched channels. "Here we go, Louis."

"I'll be ready," Bonneyman said.

"Thanks. Out." I moved up toward the head of the column. Ardwain had already gone up. "Let's get rolling," I said.

"Sir. Question, sir," Ardwain said.

"Yeah?"

"Men would rather take their packs, sir. Don't like to leave their gear behind."

"Sergeant, we've got eight kilometers to cover in less than three hours. No way."

"Yes, sir. Could we take our cloaks? Gets cold without 'em—"

"Sergeant Ardwain, we're leaving Centurion Lieberman and four maniples of troops here. Just what's going to happen to your gear? Get them marching."

"Sir. All right, you bastards, move out."

I could hear grumbling as they started along the ridge. Crazy, I thought. They want to carry packs in this.

The brush was thick, and we weren't making any progress at all. Then the scouts found a dry stream bed, and we moved into that. It was filled with boulders the size of a desk, and we hopped from one to another, moving slightly downhill. It was pitch-black, the boulders no more than shapes I could barely see. This wasn't going to work. I was already terrified.

But thank God for all that exercise in high gravity, I thought. We'll make it, but we've got to have light. I turned my set to low-power command frequency. "NCO's turn on lowest-power infrared illumination," I said. "No visible light."

I pulled the IR screen down in front of my eyes and snapped on my own IR helmet light. The boulders became pale green shapes in front of me, and I could just see them well enough to hop from one to another. Ahead of me the screen showed bright green moving splotches, my scouts and NCO's with their illuminators.

I didn't think anybody would be watching this hill with IR equipment. It didn't seem likely, and we were far from the fort where the only equipment would be—if the River Pack had any to begin with. I told myself it would take extremely good gear to spot us from farther than a klick.

Eight klicks to go and three hours to do it. Shouldn't be hard. Men are in good condition, no packs—damned fools wanted to carry them!—only rifles and ammunition. And the weapons troops, of course. They'd be slowest. Mortarmen with twenty-two kilos each to carry, and the recoilless riflemen with twenty-four.

We were sweating in no time. I opened all the vents in my armor and leathers and wondered if I ought to tell the troops to do the same. Don't be stupid, I told myself. Most of them have done this a dozen times. I can't tell them anything they don't know.

But it's my command, I kept thinking. Anything goes wrong, it's your responsibility, Hal Slater. You asked for it, too, when you took the commission.

I kept thinking of the millions of things that could go wrong. The plan didn't look nearly so good from here as it had when we were studying maps. Here we are, seventy-six men, about to try to take a fort that probably has us outnumbered. Falkenberg estimated one hundred twenty-five men in there. I'd asked him how he got the number.

"Privies, Mr. Slater. Privies. Count the number of outhouses, guess the number of bottoms per hole, and you've got a good estimate of the number of men." He hadn't even cracked a grin.

One hell of a way to guess, and Falkenberg wasn't coming along. We'd find out the hard way how accurate his estimate was.

I kept telling myself what we had going for us. The satellite photos showed nobody lived on this ridge. No privies, I thought, and grinned in the dark. But I'd gone over the pix, and I hadn't seen any signs that people were ever here. Why should they be? There was no water except for the spring inside the fort itself. There was nothing up here, not even proper firewood, only these pesky shrubs that stab at your ankles.

I came around a bend in the stream bed and found a monitor waiting. His maniple stood behind him. He had three recruits in it: one NCO, one long-term private, and three recruits. The usual organization is only one or two recruits to a maniple, and I wondered why Lieberman had set this one up this way.

The monitor motioned uphill. We had to leave the stream bed here. Far ahead of me I could see the dull green glow of my lead men's lanterns. They were pulling ahead of me, and I strained to keep up with them. I left the stream, and after a few meters the only man near me was Hartz. He struggled along with twenty kilos of communications gear on his back and a rifle in his right hand, but if he had any trouble keeping up with me, he didn't say anything. I was glad I didn't have to carry all that load.

The ridge flattened out after a hundred meters. The cover was only about waist-high. The green lights went out on my IR screen as up ahead the scouts cut their illuminators. I ordered the others turned off, as well. Then I crouched under a bush and used the map projector to show me where we were. The helmet projected the map onto the ground, a dim patch of light that couldn't have been seen except from close up and directly above.

I was surprised to see we'd come better than halfway.

Fort Beersheba hadn't been much to start with. It had a rectangle of low walls with guard towers in the corners, a miniature of the larger fort at Garrison. Then somebody had improved it, with a ditch and parapet out in front of the walls, and a concertina of rusting barbed wire outside of that. I couldn't see inside the walls, but I knew there were four above-ground buildings and three large bunkers. The buildings were adobe. The bunkers were logs and earth. They wouldn't burn. The logs were a local wood with a high metallic content.

The bunkers were going to be a problem, but they'd have to wait. Right now we had to get inside the walls of the fort. There was a gate in the wall in front of me. It was made of the same wood as the bunkers. It had a ramp across the ditch, and it looked like our best bet, except that inside the fort one of the bunkers faced the gate, and it would be able to fire through the opening once the gate was gone.

I had seventy-five men lying flat in the scrub brush three hundred meters from the fort. The place looked deserted. My IR pickups didn't show anyone in the guard towers or on the walls. Nothing. I glanced at my watch. Less than an hour before dawn.

I hadn't the faintest idea of what to do, but it was time to make up my mind.

"Don't get fancy," Falkenberg had told me. "Get the men to the fort and turn them loose. They'll take it for you."

Sure, I thought. Sure. You're not here, you bloody coward, and I am, and it's my problem, and I don't know what the hell I'm doing.

I didn't like the looks of that ditch and barbed-wire concertina. It would take a while getting through it. If we crawled up to the ditch, we'd be spotted. They couldn't be that sloppy; if there weren't any guards, there had to be a surveillance system. Body capacitance, maybe. Or radar. Something. They'd have guards posted unless they had reason to believe nobody could sneak up on them.

To hell with it. We've got to do something, I thought. I nodded to Hartz and he handed me a mike. His radio was set to a narrow-beam directional antenna, and we'd left relays along the line of sight back to the landing area. I could talk to the choppers without alerting the fort's electronic watchdogs.

"Nighthawk, this is Blackeagle," I said.

"Blackeagle go."

"We can see the place, Louis. Nothing moving at all. I'd say it was deserted if I didn't know better."

"Want me to come take a look?"

It was a thought. The chopper could circle high above the fort and scan with IR and low-light TV. We'd know who was in the open. But there was a good chance it would be spotted, and we'd throw away our best shot.

"Don't get fancy," Falkenberg had said. "Surprise—that's your big advantage. Don't blow it."

But he wasn't here. There didn't seem to be any right decision. "No," I told Louis. "That's a negative. Load up with troops and get airborne, but stay out of line of sight. Be ready to dash. When I want you, I'll want you bad."

"Aye, aye, sir."

"Blackeagle out." I gave Hartz the mike. Okay, I told myself, this is it. I waved forward to Sergeant Ardwain.

He half rose from the ground and waved. The line

moved ahead, slowly. Behind us the mortar and recoilless rifle teams had set up their weapons and lay next to them waiting for orders.

Corporal Roff was just to my left. He was directly in front of the gate. He waved his troops on and we crawled toward the gate.

We'd gotten to within a hundred meters when there appeared a light at the top of the wall by the gate. Someone up there was shining a spot out onto the field. There was another light, and then another, all hand-held spotlights, powerful, but not very wide beams.

Corporal Roff stood up and waved at them. "Hello, there!" he shouted. "Whatcha doin'?" He sounded drunk. I wanted to tell him to get down, but it was too late.

"You guys okay in there?" Roff shouted. "Got anything to drink?"

The others were crouched now, up from a crawl, and running forward.

"Who the hell are you?" someone on the wall demanded.

"Who the flippin' hell are you?" Roff answered. "Gimme a drink!" The lights converged toward him.

I thumbed on my command set. "Nighthawk, this is Blackeagle. Come a-runnin'!"

"Roger dodger."

I switched to the general channel. "Roff, hit the dirt! Fire at will. Charge!" I was shouting into the helmet radio loud enough to deafen half the command.

Roff dove sideways into the dirt. There were orange spurts from all over the field as the troopers opened fire. The lights tumbled off the walls. Two went out. One stayed on. It lay in the dirt just outside the gate.

Troopers rose from the field and ran screaming

toward the fort. They sounded like madmen. Then a light machine gun opened from behind me, then another.

Trumpet notes sounded. I hadn't ordered it. I didn't even know we had a trumpet with us. The sound seemed to spur the men on. They ran toward the wire as the mortars fired their first rounds. Seconds later I saw spurts of fire from inside the walls as the shells hit. Just as they did, the recoilless opened behind me and I heard the shell pass not more than a couple of meters to my left. It hit the gates and there was a flash, then another hit the gates, and another. The trumpeter was sounding the charge over and over again, while mortars dropped more V.T. fused to go off a meter above ground into the fort itself. The recoilless fired again.

The gates couldn't take that punishment and fell open. There was smoke inside. One of the mortarmen must have dropped smoke rounds between the gates and the bunker. Streams of tracers came out of the gates, but the men avoided them easily. They ran up on either side of the gates.

Others charged directly at the wire. The first troopers threw themselves onto the concertina. The next wave stepped on their backs and dived into the ditch. More waves followed, and men in the ditches heaved their comrades up onto the narrow strip between the ditch and the walls.

They stopped just long enough to throw grenades over the wall. Then two men grabbed a third and flung him up to where he could catch the top of the wall. They stood and boosted him on until he pulled himself up and could stand on top of it. More men followed, then leaned down to pull up their mates from below. I couldn't believe it was happening so quickly.

The men on the wire were struggling to get loose

before there was no one below to boost them over. Those were recruits, I thought. Of course. The monitors had sent the recruits first, with a simple job. Lie down and get walked on.

The helicopter came roaring in, pouring streams of twenty-mm cannon fire into the fort. The tracers were bright against the night sky.

And I was still standing there, watching, amazed at how fast it was all happening. I shook myself and turned on my command set. "I.F.F. beacons on! General order, turn on I.F.F. beacons." I changed channels. "Nighthawk, this is Blackeagle. For God's sake, Louis, be careful! Some of ours are already inside!"

"I see the beacons," Louis said. "Relax, Hal, we watched them going in."

The chopper looped around the fort in a tight orbit, still firing into the fort. Then it plunged downward.

"Mortarmen, hold up on that stuff," Sergeant Ardwain's voice said. "We're inside the fort now and the chopper's going in."

Christ, I thought, something else I forgot. One hell of a commander I've made. I can't even remember the most elementary things.

The chopper dropped low and even before it vanished behind the walls it was spewing men.

I ran up to the gate, staying to one side to avoid the tracers that were still coming out. Corporal Roff was there ahead of me. "Careful here, sir." He ducked around the gatepost and vanished. I followed him into the smoke, running around to my right, where other troopers had gone over the wall.

The scene inside was chaotic. There were unarmored bodies everywhere, probably cut down by the mortars. Men were running and firing in all directions. I didn't think any of the defenders had helmets. "Anybody without a helmet is a hostile," I said into the command set. Stupid. They know that. "Give 'em hell, lads!" That was another silly thing to say, but at least it was a better reason for shouting in their ears than telling them something they already knew.

A satchel charge went off at one of the bunkers. A squad rushed the entrance and threw grenades into it. That was all I could see from where I stood, but there was firing all over the enclosure.

Now what? I wondered. Even as I did, the firing died out until there were only a few rifle shots now and then, and the futile fire of the machine gun in the bunker covering the gate.

"Lieutenant?" It was Ardwain's voice.

"Yes, Sergeant."

"There's some people in that main bunker, sir. You can hear 'em talking in there. Sound like women. We didn't want to blow it in, not just yet, anyway."

"What about the rest of the fort?"

"Cleared out, sir. Bunkers and barracks, too. We got about twenty prisoners."

That quick. Like automatic magic. "Sergeant, make sure there's nothing that can fire onto the area northwest of the fort. I want to bring the Skyhook in there."

"Aye, aye, sir."

I thumbed my command set to the chopper frequency. "We've got the place, all except one bunker, and it'll be no problem. Bring Number Two in to land in the area northwest of the fort, about three hundred meters out from the wall. I want you to stay up there and cover Number Two. Anything that might hit it, you take care of. Keep scanning. I can't believe somebody won't come up here to see what's happening."

"Aye, aye, sir," Louis said. "Sounds like you've done some good work down there."

"We've got the place," I told him. I switched off and looked for Sergeant Ardwain. There was a lot to do, but he'd undoubtedly be doing it. I'd never felt so useless in all my life. There'd been good work done here tonight, no question about it, but I hadn't done any of it.

SEVEN

That was my first fire fight. I wasn't too proud of my part in it. I hadn't given a single order once the rush started, and I was very nearly the last man into the fort. Some leader.

But there was no time to brood. Dawn was a bright smear off in the east. The first thing was to check on the butcher's bill. Four men killed, two of them recruits. Eleven wounded. After a quick conference with our paramedic I sent three to the helicopters. The others could fight, or said they could. Then I sent the two choppers east toward Harmony, while we ferried the rest of our gear into the fort. We were on our own.

Sergeant Doc Crisp had another dozen patients, defenders who'd been wounded in the assault. We had thirty prisoners, thirty-seven wounded, and over fifty dead. One of the wounded was the former commander of the fort.

"Got bashed with a rifle butt outside his quarters," Ardwain told me. "He's able to talk now."

"I'll see him."

93

"Sir." Ardwain went into the hospital bunker and brought out a man about fifty, dark hair in a ring around a bald head. He had thin, watery eyes. He didn't look like a soldier or an outlaw.

"He says his name's Flawn, sir," Ardwain told me.

"Marines," Flawn said. "CoDominium Marines. Didn't know there were any on the planet. Just why the hell is this place worth the Grand Senate's attention again?"

"Shut up," Ardwain said.

"I've got a problem, Flawn," I said. We were standing in the open area in the center of the fort. "That bunker over there's still got some of your people in it. It'd be no problem to blast it open, but the troopers think they heard women talking in there."

"They did," Flawn said. "Our wives."

"Can you talk them into coming out, or do we set fire to it?"

"Christ!" he said. "What happens to us now?"

"*Machts nichts* to me," I told him. "My orders are to disarm you people. You're free to go anywhere you want to without weapons. Northwest if you like."

"Without weapons. You know what'll happen to us out there without weapons?"

"No, and I don't really care."

"I know," Flawn said. "You bastards never have cared—"

"Mind how you talk to the lieutenant," Ardwain said. He ground his rifle on the man's instep. Flawn gasped in pain.

"Enough of that, Sergeant," I said. "Flawn, you outlaws—"

"Outlaws. Crap!" Flawn said. "Excuse me. Sir, you are mistaken." He eyed Ardwain warily, his lip curled in contempt. "You brought me here as a convict for no reason other than my opposition to the CoDominium. You turned me loose with nothing.

Nothing at all, Lieutenant. So we try to build something. Politics here aren't like at home. Or maybe they are, same thing, really, but here it's all out in the open. I managed something, and now you've come to take it away and send me off unarmed, with no more than the clothes on my back, and you expect me to be respectful." He glanced up at the CoDominium banner that flew high above the fort. "You'll excuse me if I don't show more enthusiasm."

"My orders are to disarm you," I said. "Now, will you talk your friends out of that bunker, or do we blow it in?"

"You'll let us go?"

"Yes."

"Your word of honor, Lieutenant?"

I nodded. "Certainly."

"I guess I can't ask for any other guarantees." Flawn looked at Sergeant Ardwain and grimaced. "I wish I dared. All right, let me talk to them."

By noon we had Fort Beersheba to ourselves. Flawn and the others had left. They insisted on carrying their wounded with them, even when Doc Crisp told them most would probably die on the road. The women had been a varied assortment, from teen-agers to older women. All had gone with Flawn, to my relief and the troopers' disappointment.

Centurion Lieberman organized the defenses. He put men into the bunkers, set up revetments for the mortars, found material to repair the destroyed gates, stationed more men on the walls, got the mess tents put up, put the liquor we'd found into a strongroom and posted guards over it—

I was feeling useless again.

In another hour there were parties coming up the road. I sent Sergeant Ardwain and a squad down there to set up a roadblock. We could cover them from the fort, and the mortars were set up to spray the road. The river was about three hundred meters away and one hundred meters below us, and the fort had a good field of fire all along the road for a klick in either direction. It was easy to see why this bluff had been chosen for a strong point.

As parties of refugees came through, Ardwain disarmed them. At first they went through, anyway, but after a while they began to turn back rather than surrender their weapons. None of them caused any problems, and I wouldn't let Ardwain pursue any that turned away. We had far too few men to risk any in something senseless like that.

"Good work," Falkenberg told me when I made the afternoon report. "We've made forty kilometers so far, and we've got a couple of hours of daylight left. It's a bit hard to estimate how fast we'll be able to march."

"Yes, sir. The first party we disarmed had three Skyhawk missiles. There were five here at the fort, but nobody got them out in time to use them. Couple of guys who tried were killed by the mortars. It doesn't look good for helicopters in this area, though, not now that they're warned."

"Yes," Falkenberg said. "I suspected as much. We'll retire the choppers for a while. You've done well, Slater. I caution you not to relax, though. At the moment we've had no opposition worth mentioning, but that will change soon enough, and after that there may be an effort to break past your position. They don't seem to want to give up their weapons."

"No, sir." And who can blame them? I thought. Eric Flawn had worried me. He hadn't seemed like an outlaw. I don't know what I'd expected here at Beersheba. Kidnapped girls. Scenes of rape and debauchery, I suppose. I'd never seen a thieves' government in operation. Certainly I hadn't expected what I'd found, a group of middle-aged men in control of troops who looked a lot like ours, only theirs weren't very well equipped.

"I understand you liberated some wine," Falkenberg said.

"Yes, sir."

"That'll help. Daily ration of no more than half a liter per man, though."

"Sir? I wasn't planning on giving them any of it until you got here."

"It's theirs, Slater," Falkenberg said. "You could get away with holding on to it, but it wouldn't be best. It's your command. Do as you think you should, but if you want advice, give the troops half a liter each."

"Yes, sir." There's no regulation against drinking in the Line Marines, not even on duty. There are severe penalties for rendering yourself unfit for duty. Men have even been shot for it. "Half a liter with supper, then."

"I think it's wise," Falkenberg said. "Well, sounds as if you're doing well. We'll be along in a few days. Out."

There were a million other details. At noon I'd been startled to hear a trumpet sound mess call, and I went out to see who was doing it. A corporal I didn't recognize had a polished brass trumpet.

"Take me a few days to get everyone's name straight, Corporal," I said. "Yours?"

"Corporal Brady, sir."

"You play that well."

"Thank you, sir."

I looked at him again. I was sure his face was familiar. I thought I remembered that he'd been on Tri-v. Had his own band and singing group. Nightclub performances, at least one Tri-v special. I won-

dered what he was doing as an enlisted man in the
Line Marines, but I couldn't ask. I tried to remember his real name, but that escaped me, too. It hadn't
been Brady, I was sure of that. "You'll be sounding
all calls here?"

"Yes, sir. Centurion says I'm to do it."

"Right. Carry on, Brady."

All through the afternoon the trumpet calls sent
men to other duties. An hour before the evening
meal there was a formal retreat. The CoDominium
banner was hauled down by a color guard while all
the men not on sentry watch stood in formation and
Brady played Colors. As they folded the banner I
remembered a lecture in Leadership class back at
the Academy.

The instructor had been a dried-up Marine major
with one real and one artificial arm. We were supposed to guess which was which, but we never did.
The lecture I remembered had been on ceremonials.
"Always remember," he'd said, "the difference between an army and a mob is tradition and discipline.
You cannot enforce discipline on troops who do not
feel that they are being justly treated. Even the man
who is wrongly punished must feel that what he is
accused of deserves punishment. You cannot enforce
discipline on a mob, and so your men must be reminded that they are soldiers. Ceremonial is one of
your most powerful tools for doing that. It is true
that we are perpetually accused of wasting money.
The Grand Senate annually wishes to take away our
dress uniforms, our badges and colors, and all the
so-called non-functional items we employ. They are
fortunate, because they have never been able to do
that. The day that they do, they will find themselves
with an army that cannot defend them.

"Soldiers will complain about ceremonials and spit-
and-polish, and such like, but they cannot live as an

army without them. Men fight for pride, not for money, and no service that does not give them pride will last very long."

Maybe, I thought. But with a thousand things to do, I could have passed up a formal retreat on our first day at Fort Beersheba. I hadn't been asked about it. By the time I knew it was to happen, Lieberman had made all the arrangements and given the orders.

By suppertime we were organized for the night. Ardwain had collected about a hundred weapons, mostly obsolete rifles—there were even muzzle-loaders, hand-made here on Arrarat—and passed nearly three hundred people through the roadblock.

We closed the road at dusk. Searchlights played along it, and we had a series of roadblocks made of log stacks. Ardwain and his troops were dug in where they could cover the whole road area, and we could cover them from the fort. It looked pretty good.

Tattoo sounded, and Fort Beersheba began to settle in for the night.

I made my rounds, looking into everything. The body-capacitance system the previous occupants had relied on was smashed when we blew open their bunker, but we'd brought our own surveillance gear. I didn't really trust passive systems, but I needn't have worried. Lieberman had guards in each of the towers. They were equipped with light-amplifying binoculars. There were more men to watch the IR screens.

"We're safe enough," Lieberman said. "If the lieutenant would care to turn in, I'll see the guard's changed properly."

He followed me back to my quarters. Hartz had already fixed the place up. There were fresh adobe patches over the bullet holes in the walls. My gear was laid out where I could get it quickly. Hartz had his cloak and pack spread out in the anteroom.

There was even coffee. A pot was kept warm over an alcohol lamp.

"You can leave it to us," Lieberman said.

Hartz grinned. "Sure. Lieutenants come out of the Academy without any calluses, and we make generals out of them."

"That may take some doing," I said. I invited Lieberman into my sitting room. There was a table there, with a scale model of the fort on it. Flawn had made it, but it hadn't done him much good. "Have a seat, Centurion. Coffee?"

"Just a little, sir. I'd best get back to my duties."

"Call me for the next watch, Centurion."

"If the lieutenant orders it."

"I just—what the hell, Lieberman, why don't you want me to take my turn on guard?"

"No need, sir. May I make a suggestion?"

"Sure."

"Leave it to us, sir. We know what we're doing."

I nodded and stared into my coffee cup. I didn't feel I was really in command here. They tell you everything in the Academy: leadership, communications, the precise form of a regimental parade, laser range-finding systems, placement of patches on uniforms, how to compute firing patterns for mortars, wine rations for the troops, how to polish a pair of boots, servicing recoilless rifles, delivery of calling cards to all senior officers within twenty-four hours of reporting to a new post, assembly and maintenance of helicopters, survival on rocks with poisonous atmosphere or no atmosphere at all, shipboard routines, and a million other details. You have to learn them all, and they get mixed up until you don't know what's trivial and what's important. They're just things you have to know to pass examinations. "You know what you're doing, Centurion, but I'm not sure I do."

"Sir, I've noticed something about young officers," Lieberman said. "They all take things too serious."

"Command's a serious business." Damn, I thought. That's pompous. Especially from a young kid to an older soldier.

He didn't take in that way. "Yes, sir. Too damned serious to let details get in the way. Lieutenant, if it was just things like posting the guard and organizing the defense of this place, the service wouldn't need officers. We can take care of all that. What we need is somebody to tell us what the hell to do. Once that's done, we know *how*."

I didn't say anything. He looked at me closely, probably trying to figure out if I was angry. He didn't seem very worried.

"Take me, for instance," he said. "I don't know why the hell we came to this place, and I don't care. Everybody's got his reasons for joining up. Me, I don't know what else to do. I've found something I'm good at, and I can do it. Officers tell me where to fight, and that's one less damn thing to worry about."

The trumpet sounded outside. Last Post. It was the second time we'd heard it today. The first was when we'd buried our dead.

"Got my rounds to make," Lieberman said. "By your leave, sir."

"Carry on, Centurion." A few minutes later Hartz came in to help me get my boots off. He wouldn't hear of letting me turn in wearing them.

"We'll hold 'em off long enough to get your boots on, zur. Nobody's going to catch a Marine officer in the sack."

He'd sleep with his boots on so that I could take mine off. It didn't make a lot of sense, but I wasn't going to win any arguments with him about it. I rolled into the sack and stared at the ceiling. My first day of command. I was still thinking about that when I went to sleep.

The attacks started the next day. At first it was just small parties trying to force the roadblock, and they never came close to doing that. We could put too much fire onto them from the fort.

That night they tried the fort itself. There were a dozen mortars out there. They weren't very accurate, and our radar system worked fine. They would get off a couple of rounds, and then we'd have them backtracked to the origin point and our whole battery would drop in on them. We couldn't silence them completely, but we could make it unhealthy for the crews servicing their mortars, and after a while the fire slackened. There were rifle attacks all through the night, but nothing in strength.

"Just testing you," Falkenberg said in the morning when I reported to him. "We're pressing hard from this end. They'll make a serious try before long."

"Yes, sir. How are things at your end?"

"We're moving," Falkenberg said. "There's more resistance than the colonel expected, of course. With you stopping up their bolt hole, they've got no route to retreat through. Fight or give up—that's all the choice we left them. You can look for their real effort to break past you in a couple of days. By then we'll be close enough to really worry them."

He was right. By the fourth day we were under continuous attack from more than a thousand hostiles.

It was a strange situation. No one was really worried. We were holding them off. Our ammunition stocks were running low, but Lieberman's answer to that was to order the recruits to stop using their weapons. They were put to serving mortars and re-coilless rifles, with an experienced NCO in charge to make sure there was a target worth the effort before they fired. The riflemen waited for good shots and made each one count.

As long as the ammunition held out, we were in no serious danger. The fort had a clear field of fire, and we weren't faced by heavy artillery. The best the enemy had was mortars, and our counterbattery radar and computer system was more than a match for that.

"No discipline," Lieberman said. "They got no discipline. Come in waves, run in waves, but they never press the attack. Damned glad there's no Marine deserters in that outfit. They'd have broke through if they'd had good leadership."

"I'm worried about our ammunition supplies," I said.

"Hell, Lieutenant, Cap'n Falkenberg will get here. He's never let anybody down yet."

"You've served with him before?"

"Yes, sir, in that affair on Domingo. Christian Johnny, we called him. He'll be here."

Everyone acted that way. It made the situation unreal. We were under fire. You couldn't put your head above the wall or outside the gate. Mortars dropped in at random intervals, sometimes catching men in the open and wounding them despite their body armor. We had four dead and nine more in the hospital bunker. We were running low on ammunition, and we faced better than ten-to-one odds, and nobody was worried.

"Your job is to look confident," Falkenberg had told me. Sure.

On the fifth day things were getting serious for Sergeant Ardwain and his men at the roadblock. They were running out of ammunition and water.

"Abandon it, Ardwain," I told him. "Bring your troops up here. We can keep the road closed with fire from the fort."

"Sir. I have six casualties that can't walk, sir."

"How many total?"

"Nine, sir—two walking and one dead."

Nine out of a total of twelve men. "Hold fast, Sergeant. We'll come get you."

"Aye, aye, sir."

I wondered who I could spare. There wasn't much doubt as to who was the most useless man on the post. I sent for Lieberman.

"Centurion, I want a dozen volunteers to go with me to relieve Ardwain's group. We'll take full packs and extra ammunition and supplies."

"Lieutenant—"

"Damn it, don't tell me you don't want me to go. You're capable enough. You told me that you need officers to tell you what to do, not how to do it. Fine. Your orders are to hold this post until Falkenberg comes. One last thing—you will not send or take any relief forces down the hill. I won't have this command further weakened. Is that understood?"

"Sir."

"Fine. Now get me a dozen volunteers."

I decided to go down the hill just after moonset. We got the packs loaded and waited at the gate. One of my volunteers was Corporal Brady. He stood at the gate, chatting with the sentry there.

"Quiet tonight," Brady said.

"They're still there, though," the sentry said. "You'll know soon enough. Bet you tomorrow's wine ration you don't make it down the hill."

"Done. Remember, you said *down* the hill. I expect you to save that wine for me."

"Yeah. Hey, this is a funny place, Brady."

"How's that?"

"A holy Joe planet, and no Marine chaplain."

"You want a chaplain?"

The sentry shrugged. He had a huge black beard that he fingered, as if feeling for lice. "Good idea, isn't it?"

"They're all right, but we don't need a chaplain. What we need is a good Satanist. No Satanist in this battalion."

"What do you need one of them for?"

Brady laughed. "Stands to reason, don't it? God's good, right? He'll treat you okay. It's the other guy you have to watch out for." He laughed again. "Got three days on bread and no wine for saying that once. Told it to Chaplain Major McCrory, back at Sector H.Q. He didn't appreciate it."

"Time to move out," I said. I shouldered my heavy pack.

"Do we run or walk, zur?" Hartz asked.

"Walk until they know we're there. And be quiet about it."

"Zur."

"Move out, Brady. Quietly."

"Sir." The sentry opened the gate, just a crack. Brady went through, then another trooper, and another. Nothing happened, and finally it was my turn. Hartz was last in the line.

The trail led steeply down the side of the cliff. It was about two meters wide, just a slanting ledge, really. We were halfway down when there was a burst of machine-gun fire. One of the troopers went down.

"Move like hell!" I said.

Two men grabbed the fallen trooper and hauled him along. We ran down the cliff face, jumping across shortcuts at the switchbacks. There was nothing we could see to shoot at, but more bullets sent chips flying from the granite cliff.

The walls above us spurted flame. It looked like the whole company was up there covering us. I hoped not. One of our recoilless men found a target and for a few moments we weren't under fire. Then the rifles opened up. Something zinged past my ear. Then I felt a hard punch in the gut and went down.

I lay there sucking air. Hartz grabbed one arm and shouted to another private. "Jersey! Lieutenant's down. Give me a hand."

"I'm all right," I said. I felt my stomach area. There wasn't any blood. "Armor stopped it. Just knocked the wind out of me." I was still gasping, and I couldn't get my breath.

They dragged me along to Ardwain's command post. "How would we explain to the Centurion if we didn't get you down?" Hartz asked.

The CP was a trench roofed over with ironwood logs. There were three wounded men at one end. Brady took our wounded trooper there. He'd been hit in both legs. Brady put tourniquets on them.

Hartz had his own ideas about first aid. He had a brandy flask. It was supposed to be a universal cure. After he poured two shots down me, he went over to the other end of the bunker to pass the bottle among the other wounded.

"Only three of them, Ardwain?" I said. I was still gasping for air. "I thought you had six."

"Six who cannot walk, sir. But three of them can still fight."

EIGHT

"We're not going to get up that bluff. Not carrying wounded," I said.

"No, sir." Ardwain had runners carrying ammunition to his troopers. "We're dug in good, sir. With the reinforcements you brought, we'll hold out."

"We damned well have to," I said.

"Not so bad, sir. Most of our casualties came from recoilless and mortars. They've stopped using them. Probably low on ammunition."

"Let's hope they stay that way." I had another problem. The main defense for the roadblock was mortar fire from the fort. Up above they were running low on mortar shells. In another day we'd be on our own. No point in worrying about it, I decided. We'll just have to do the best we can.

The next day was the sixth we'd been in the fort. We were low on rations. Down at the roadblock we had nothing to eat but a dried meat that the men called "monkey." It didn't taste bad, but it had the peculiar property of expanding when you chewed it, so that after a while it seemed as if you had a mouthful of rubber bands. It was said that Line Marines could march a thousand kilometers if they had coffee, wine, and monkey.

We reached Falkenberg by radio at noon. He was still forty kilometers away, and facing the hardest fighting yet. They had to go through villages practically house by house.

"Can you hold?" he asked me.

"The rest of today and tonight, easily. By noon tomorrow we'll be out of mortar shells. Sooner, maybe. When that happens, our outpost down at the road-block will be without support." I hadn't told him where I was.

"Can you hold until 1500 hours tomorrow?" he asked.

"The fort will hold. Don't know about the road-block."

"We'll see what we can do," Falkenberg said. "Good luck."

"Christian Johnny'll get us out," Brady said.

"You know him?"

"Yes, sir. He'll get us out."

I wished I were as sure as he was.

They tried infiltrating during the night. I don't know how many crept up along the riverbank, but there were a lot of them. Some went on past us. The others moved in on our bunkers. The fighting was hand to hand, with knives and bayonets and grenades doing most of the work, until we got our foxholes clear and I was able to order the men down into them. Then I had Lieberman drop mortar fire in on our own positions for ten minutes. When it lifted, we went out to clear the area.

When morning came we had three more dead, and every man in the section was wounded. I'd got a grenade fragment in my left upper arm just below where the armor left off. It was painful, but nothing to worry about.

There were twenty dead in our area, and bloody trails were leading off where more enemies had crawled away.

An hour after dawn they rushed us again. The fort had few mortar shells left. We called each one in carefully. They couldn't spare us too much attention, though, because there was a general attack on the fort, as well. When there were moments of quiet in the firing around Fort Beersheba, we could hear more distant sounds to the east. Falkenberg's column was blasting its way through another village.

Ardwain got it just at noon. A rifle bullet in the neck. It looked bad. Brady dragged him into the main bunker and put a compress on. Ardwain's breath rattled in his throat, and his mouth oozed blood. That left Roff and Brady as NCO's, and Roff was immobile, with fragments through his left leg.

At 1230 hours we had four effectives, and no fire support from the fort. We'd lost the troops down by the riverbank, and we could hear movement there.

"They're getting past us, damn it!" I shouted. "All this for nothing! Hartz, get me Lieberman."

"Zur." Hartz was working one-handed. His right arm was in shreds. He insisted on staying with me, but I didn't count him as one of my effectives.

"Sergeant Roszak," the radio said.

"Where's Lieberman?"

"Dead, sir. I'm senior NCO."

"What mortar ammunition have you?"

"Fourteen rounds, sir."

"Drop three onto the riverbank just beyond us, and stand by to use more."

"Aye, aye, sir. One moment." There was silence. Then he said, "On the way."

"How is it up there?"

"We're fighting at the walls, sir. We've lost the north section, but the bunkers are covering that area."

"Christ. You'll need the mortars to hold the fort. But there's no point in holding that fort if the roadblock goes. Stand by to use the last mortar rounds at my command."

"Aye, aye, sir. We can hold."

"Sure you can." Sure.

I looked out through the bunker's firing slit. There were men coming up the road. Dozens of them. I had one clip left in my rifle, and I began trying to pick them off with slow fire. Hartz used his rifle with his left hand, firing one shot every two seconds, slow, aimed fire.

There were more shots from off to my left. Corporal Brady was in a bunker over there, but his radio wasn't working. Attackers moved toward his position. I couldn't hear any others of my command.

Suddenly Brady's trumpet sounded. The brassy notes cut through the battle noises. He played "To Arms!," then settled into the Line Marine march. "We've left blood in the dirt of twenty-five worlds—"

There was a movement in the bunker. Recruit Dietz, hit twice in the stomach, had dragged himself over to Sergeant Ardwain and found Ardwain's pistol. He crawled up to the firing slit and began shooting. He coughed blood with each round. Another trooper staggered out of the bush. He reeled like a drunk as he lurched toward the road. He carried a sack of grenades strung around his neck and threw them mechanically, staggering forward and throwing grenades. He had only one arm. He was hit a dozen times and fell, but his arm moved to throw the last grenade before he died.

More attackers moved toward Brady's bunker. The

trumpet call wavered for a moment as Brady fired, and then the notes came as clear as ever.

"Roszak! I've got a fire mission," I said.

"Sir."

"Let me describe the situation down here." I gave him the positions of my CP, Brady's bunker, and the only other one I thought might have any of our troops in it. "Everyplace else is full of hostiles, and they're getting past us along the riverbank. I want you to drop a couple of mortar rounds forty meters down the road from the CP, just north of the road, but not too far north. Corporal Brady's in there and it would be a shame to spoil his concert."

"We hear him up here, sir. Wait one." There was silence. "On the way."

The mortar shells came in seconds later. Brady was still playing. I remembered his name now. It was ten years ago on Earth. He'd been a famous man until he dropped out of sight. Roszak had left his mike open, and in the background I could hear the men in the fort cheering wildly.

Roszak's voice came in my ears. "General order from battalion headquarters, sir. You're to stay in your bunkers. No one to expose himself. Urgent general order, sir."

I wondered what the hell Falkenberg was doing giving me general orders, but I used my command set to pass them along. I doubted if anyone heard, but it didn't matter. No one was going anywhere.

Suddenly the road exploded. The whole distance from fifty meters away down as far as I could see vanished in a line of explosions. They kept coming, pounding the road; then the riverbank was lifted in great clods of mud. The road ahead was torn to bits; then the pieces were lifted by another salvo, and another. I dove into the bottom of the bunker and held my ears while shells dropped all around me.

Finally it lifted. I could hear noises in my phones, but my ears were ringing, and I couldn't understand. It wasn't Roszak's voice. Finally it came through. "Do you need more fire support, Mr. Slater?"

"No. Lord, what shooting—"

"I'll tell the gunners that," Falkenberg said. "Hang on, Hal. We'll be another hour, but you'll have fire support from now on."

Outside, Brady's trumpet sang out another march.

NINE

They sent me back to Garrison to get my arm fixed.
There's a fungus infection on Arrarat that makes
even minor wounds dangerous. I spent a week in
surgery getting chunks cut out of my arm, then
another week in regeneration stimulation. I wanted
to get back to my outfit, but the surgeon wouldn't
hear of it. He wanted me around to check up on the
regrowth.

Sergeant Ardwain was in the next bay. It was
going to take a while to get him back together, but
he'd be all right. With Lieberman dead, Ardwain
would be up for a Centurion's badges.

It drove me crazy to be in Garrison while my
company, minus its only officer and both its senior
NCO's, was out at Fort Beersheba. The day they let
me out of sick bay I was ready to mutiny, but there
wasn't any transportation, and Major Lorca made it
clear that I was to stay in Garrison until the surgeon
released me. I went to my quarters in a blue funk.

The place was all fixed up. Private Hartz was there
grinning at me. His right arm was in an enormous

cast, bound to his chest with what seemed like a mile of gauze.

"How did you get out before I did?" I asked him.

"No infection, zur. I poured brandy on the wounds." He winced. "It was a waste, but there was more than enough for the few of us left."

There was another surprise. Irina Swale came out of my bedroom.

"Miss Swale has been kind enough to help with the work here, zur," Hartz said. He seemed embarrassed. "She insisted, zur. If the lieutenant will excuse me, I have laundry to pick up, zur."

I grinned at him and he left. Now what? I wondered. "Thanks."

"It's the least I could do for Arrarat's biggest hero," Irina said.

"Hero? Nonsense—"

"I suppose it's nonsense that my father is giving you the military medal, and that Colonel Harrington has put in for something else; I forget what, but it can't be approved here—it has to come from Sector Headquarters."

"News to me," I said. "And I still don't think—"

"You don't have to. Aren't you going to ask me to sit down? Would you like something to drink? We have everything here. Private Hartz is terribly efficient."

"So are you. I'm not doing well, am I? Please have a seat. I'd get you a drink, but I don't know where anything is."

"And you couldn't handle the bottles, anyway. I'll get it." She went into the other room and came out with two glasses. Brandy for me and that Jericho wine she liked. Hartz at work, I thought. I'll be drinking that damned brandy the rest of my life.

"It was pretty bad, wasn't it?" she said. She sat on the couch that had appeared while I was gone.

"Bad enough." Out of my original ninety, there were only twelve who hadn't been wounded. Twenty-eight dead, and another dozen who wouldn't be back on duty for a long time. "But we held." I shook my head. "Not bragging, Irina. Amazed, mostly. We held."

"I've been wondering about something," she said. "I asked Louis Bonneyman, and he wouldn't answer me. Why did you have to hold the fort? It was much the hardest part of the campaign, wasn't it? Why didn't Captain Falkenberg do it?"

"Had other things to do, I suppose. They haven't let me off drugs long enough to learn anything over in sick bay. What's happening out there?"

"It went splendidly," she said. "The Harmony militia are in control of the whole river. The boats are running again, grain prices have fallen here in the city—"

"You don't sound too happy."

"Is it that obvious?" She sat quietly for a moment. She seemed to be trying to control her face. Her lip was trembling. "My father says you've accomplished your mission. He won't let Colonel Harrington send you out to help the other farmers. And the River Pack weren't the worst of the convict governments! In a lot of ways they weren't even so bad. I thought . . . I'd hoped you could go south, to the farmlands, where things are really bad, but Hugo has negotiated a steady supply of grain and he says it's none of our business."

"You're certainly anxious to get us killed."

She looked at me furiously. Then she saw my grin. "By the way," she said, "you're expected at the palace for dinner tonight. I've already cleared it with the surgeon. And this time I expect you to come! All those plans for my big party, and it was nothing but a trick your Captain Falkenberg had planned! You will come, won't you? Please?"

We ate alone. Governor Swale was out in the newly taken territory trying to set up a government that would last. Irina's mother had left him years before, and her only brother was a Navy officer somewhere in Pleiades Sector.

After dinner I did what she probably expected me to. I kissed her, then held her close to me and hoped to go to something a bit more intimate. She pushed me away. "Hal, please."

"Sorry."

"Don't be. I like you, Hal. It's just that—"

"Deane Knowles," I said.

She gave me a puzzled look. "No, of course not. But . . . I do like your friend Louis. Can't we be friends, Hal? Do we have to—"

"Of course we can be friends."

I saw a lot of her in the next three weeks. Friends. I found myself thinking about her when I wasn't with her, and I didn't like that. The whole thing's silly, I told myself. Junior officers have no business getting involved with Governors' daughters. Nothing can come of it, and you don't want anything to come of it to begin with. Your life's complicated enough as it is.

I kept telling myself that right up to the day the surgeon told me I could rejoin my outfit. I was glad to go.

It was still my company. I hadn't been with most of them at all, and I'd been with the team at the fort only a few days, but A Company was mine. Every man in the outfit thought so. I wondered what I'd done right. It didn't seem to me that I'd made any good decisions, or really any at all.

"Luck," Deane told me. "They think you're lucky."

That explained it. Line Marines are probably the most superstitious soldiers in history. And we'd certainly had plenty of luck.

I spent the next six weeks honing the troops into shape. By that time Ardwain was back, with Centurion's badges. He was posted for light duty only, but that didn't stop him from working the troops until they were ready to drop. We had more recruits, recently arrived convicts, probably men who'd been part of the River Pack at one time. It didn't matter. The Marine Machine takes over, and if it doesn't break you, you come out a Marine.

Falkenberg had a simple solution to the problem of deserters. He offered a reward, no questions asked, to anyone who brought in a deserter—and a larger reward for anyone bringing in the deserter's head. It wasn't an original idea, but it was effective.

Or had been effective. As more weeks went by with nothing to do but make patrols along the river, drill and train, stand formal retreat and parades and inspections, men began to think of running.

They also went berserk. They'd get drunk and shoot a comrade. Steal. We couldn't drill them forever, and when we gave them any time off, they'd get the bug.

The day the main body had reached Fort Beersheba, the 501st had been combat-weary, with a quarter of its men on the casualty list. It was an exhausted battalion, but it had high spirits. Now, a few months later, it was up to strength, trained to perfection, well organized and well fed—and unhappy.

I found a trooper painting I.H.T.F.P. on the orderly room wall. He dropped the paint bucket and stood to attention as I came up.

"And what does that mean, Hora?"

He stood straight as a ramrod. "Sir, it means 'I Have Truly Found Paradise.' "

"And what's going to happen to you if Sergeant Major truly finds Private Hora painting on the orderly room wall?"

"Cells, Lieutenant."

"If you're lucky. More likely you'll get to dig a hole and live in it a week. Hora, I'm going to the club for a drink. I don't expect to see any paint on that wall when I come back."

Deane laughed when I told him about it. "So they're doing that already. 'I hate this fucking place.' He means it, too."

"Give us another six weeks and I'll be painting walls," I said. "Only I'll put mine on the Governor's palace."

"You'll have to wait your turn," Deane said.

"Goddamn it, Deane, what can we do? The NCO's have gotten so rough I think I'll have to start noticing it, but if we relax discipline at all, things will really come apart."

"Yeah. Have you spoken to Falkenberg about it?"

"Sure I have," I told him. "But what can he do? What we need is some combat, Deane. I never thought I'd say that. I thought that was all garbage that they gave us at the Academy, that business about *le cafard* and losing more men to it than to an enemy, but I believe it now."

"Cheer up," Deane said. "Louis is officer of the day, and I just heard the word from him. We've got a break in the routine. Tomorrow Governor Hugo Swale, Hisself, is coming to pay a visit to the gallant troops of the 501st. He's bringing your medal, I make no doubt."

"How truly good," I said. "I'd rather he brought us a good war."

"Give him time," Deane said. "The way those damned merchants from Harmony are squeezing the farmers, they're all ready to revolt."

"Just what we need. A campaign to put down the farmers," I said. "Poor bastards. They get it from everybody, don't they? Convicts that call themselves tax collectors. Now you say the Harmony merchants—"

"Yeah," Deane said. "Welcome to the glory of CoDominium Service."

Sergeant Major Ogilvie's baritone rang out across the Fort Beersheba parade ground. "Battalion, *atten-hut!* A Company color guard, front and center, *march!*"

That was a surprise. Governor Swale had just presented me with the military medal, which isn't the Earth, but I was a bit proud of it. Now our color guard marched across the hard adobe field to the reviewing stand.

"Attention to orders," Ogilvie said. "For conspicuous gallantry in the face of the enemy, A Company, 501st Provisional Battalion, is awarded the Unit Citation of Merit. By order of Rear Admiral Sergei Lermontov, Captain of the Fleet, Crucis Sector Headquarters. A Company, *pass in review!*"

Bits of cloth and metal, and men will die for them, I thought. The old military game. It's all silly. And we held our heads high as we marched past the reviewing stand.

Falkenberg had found five men who could play bagpipes, or claimed they could—how can you tell if they're doing it right?—and they had made their own pipes. Now they marched around the table in the officers' mess at Fort Beersheba. Stewards brought whiskey and brandy.

Governor Hugo Swale sat politely, trying not to show any distress as the pipers thundered past him. Eventually they stopped. "I think we should join the ladies," Swale said. He looked relieved when Falkenberg stood.

We went into the lounge. Irina had brought another girl, a visitor from one of the farm areas. She was about nineteen, I thought, with red-brown hair and blue eyes. She would have been beautiful if she didn't have a perpetual haunted look. Irina had introduced her as Kathryn Malcolm.

Governor Swale was obviously embarrassed to have her around. He was a strange little man. There was no resemblance between him and Irina, nothing that would make you think he was her father. He was short and dumpy, almost completely bald, with wrinkles on his high forehead. He had a quick nervous manner of speaking and gesturing. He so obviously disliked Kathryn that I think only the bagpipes could have driven him to want to get back to her company. I wondered why. There'd been no chance to talk to any of them at dinner.

We sat around the fireplace. Falkenberg gave a curt nod, and all the stewards left except Monitor Lazar, Falkenberg's own orderly. Lazar brought a round of drinks and went off into the pantry.

"Well. Here's to A Company and its commander," Falkenberg said. I sat embarrassed as the others stood and lifted their glasses.

"Good work, indeed," Hugo Swale said. "Thanks to this young man, the Jordan Valley is completely pacified. It will take a long time before there's any buildup of arms here again. I want to thank you gentlemen for doing such a thorough job."

I'd had a bit too much to drink with dinner, and there'd been brandy afterward, and the pipers with their wild war sounds. My head was buzzing. "Perhaps too thorough," I muttered as the others sat down. I honestly don't know whether I wanted the others to hear me or not. Deane and Louis threw me sharp looks.

"What do you mean, Hal?" Irina asked.

"Nothing."

"Spit it out," Falkenberg said. The tone made it an order.

"I've a dozen good men in cells and three more in a worse kind of punishment, half my company is on extra duty, and the rest of them are going slowly mad," I said. "If we'd left a bit of the fighting to do, we'd at least have employment." I tried to make it a joke.

Governor Swale took it seriously. "It's as much a soldier's job to prevent trouble as to fight," he said.

You pompous ass, I thought. But of course he was right.

"There's plenty that needs doing," Kathryn Malcolm said. "If your men are spoiling to fight somebody, loan them to us for a while." She wasn't joking at all.

Governor Swale wasn't pleased at all. "That will do, Kathryn. You know we can't do that."

"And why not?" she demanded. "You're supposed to be Governor of this whole planet, but the only people you care about are the merchants in Harmony—those sanctimonious hymn-singers! You know the grain they're buying is stolen. Stolen from us, by gangsters who claim to be our government, and if we don't give them what they want, they take it anyway, and kill everyone who tries to stop them. And then you buy it from them!"

"There is nothing I can do," Swale protested. "I don't have enough troops to govern the whole planet. The Grand Senate explicitly instructed me to deal with local governments—"

"The way you did with the River Pack," Kathryn said. Her voice was bitter. "All they did was try to make some money by charging tolls for river traffic. They wouldn't deal with your damned merchants, so you sent the Marines to bargain with them. Just how many people in the Jordan Valley thanked you for that, Governor? Do they think you're their liberator?"

"Kathryn, that's not fair," Irina protested. "There are plenty of people glad to be free of the River Pack. You shouldn't say things like that."

"All I meant was that the River Pack wasn't so bad. Not compared to what *we* have to live with. But his Excellency isn't concerned about us, because his merchants can buy their grain at low prices. He doesn't care that we've become slaves."

Swale's lips tightened, but he didn't say anything.

"Local governments," Kathryn said. "What you've done, Governor, is recognize one gang. There's another gang, too, and both of them collect taxes from us! It's bad enough with just one, but it can't even protect us from the other! If you won't give us our land back, can't you at least put down the rival gangsters so we only have one set of crooks stealing from us?"

Swale kept his voice under control. He was elaborately polite as he said, "There is nothing we can do, Miss Malcolm. I wish there were. I suggest you people help yourselves."

"That isn't fair, either," Irina said. "You know it isn't. They didn't ask for all those convicts to be sent here. I think Kathryn has a very good idea. Loan her the 501st. Once those hills are cleaned out and the gangsters are disarmed, the farmers can protect themselves. Can't they, Kathryn?"

"I think so. We'd be ready, this time."

"See? And Hal says his men are spoiling for a good fight. Why not let them do it?"

"Irina, I have to put up with that from Miss Malcolm because she is a guest, but I do not have to take it from you, and I will not. Captain, I thought I was an invited guest on this post."

Falkenberg nodded. "I think we'd best change the subject," he said.

There was an embarrassed silence. Then Kathryn got up and went angrily to the door. "You needn't bother to see me to my room," she said. "I can take care of myself. I've had to do it often enough. I'm not surprised that Captain Falkenberg isn't eager to lead his troops into the hills. I notice that he sent a newly commissioned lieutenant to do the tough part of Governor Swale's dirty work. I'm not surprised at all that he doesn't want any more fighting." She left, slamming the door behind her.

Falkenberg acted as if he hadn't heard her. I don't suppose there was anything else he could do. The party didn't last much longer.

I went to my rooms alone. Deane and Louis offered to stay with me, but I didn't want them. I told them I'd had enough celebrating.

Hartz had left the brandy bottle on the table, and I poured myself another drink, although I didn't want it. The table was Arrarat ironwood, and God knows how the troops had managed to cut planks out of it. My company had built it, and a desk, and some other furniture, and put them in my rooms while I was in hospital. I ran my hand along the polished tabletop.

She should never have said that, I thought. And I expect it's my fault. I remembered Irina saying much the same thing back in Garrison, and I hadn't protested. My damned fault. Falkenberg never explained anything about himself, and I'd never learned why he hadn't come with us the night we attacked the fort, but I was damned sure it wasn't cowardice. Louis and Deane had straightened me out about that. No one who'd been with him on the march up the river could even suspect it.

And why the hell didn't I tell Irina that? I wondered. Cocky kid, trying to impress the girl. Too busy being proud of himself to—

There was a knock on the door. "Come in," I said.

It was Sergeant Major Ogilvie. There were some others in the hall. "Yes, Sergeant Major?"

"If we could have a word with the lieutenant. We have a problem, sir."

"Come in."

Ogilvie came inside. When his huge shoulders were out of the doorway, I saw Monitor Lazar and Kathryn Malcolm behind him. They all came in, and Kathryn stood nervously, her hands twisted together. "It's all my fault," she said.

Ogilvie ignored her. "Sir, I have to report that Monitor Lazar has removed certain orders from the battalion files without authorization."

"Why tell me?" I asked. "He's Captain Falkenberg's orderly."

"Sir, if you'll look at the papers. He showed them to this civilian. If you say we should report it to the captain, we'll have to." Ogilvie's voice was carefully controlled. He handed me a bound stack of papers.

They were orders from Colonel Harrington to Falkenberg as commander of the 501st, and they were dated the first day we'd arrived on Arrarat. I'd never seen them myself. No reason I should, unless Falkenberg were killed and I had to take over as his deputy.

Lazar stood at rigid attention. He wasn't looking at me, but seemed fascinated with a spot on the wall above me.

"You say Miss Malcom has read these, Sergeant Major?"

"Yes, sir."

"Then it will do no harm if I read them, I suppose." I opened the order book. The first pages were general orders commanding Falkenberg to organize the 501st. There was more, about procedures for liaison with Major Lorca and the Garrison supply depot. I'd seen copies of all those. "Why the devil did you think Miss Malcolm would be interested in this stuff, Lazar?" I asked.

"Not that, sir," Ogilvie said. "Next page."

I thumbed through the book again. There it was.

Captain John Christian Falkenberg, Commanding Officer, 501st Provisional Battalion of Line Marines:

1. These orders are written confirmation of verbal orders issued in conference with above-named officer.
2. The 50lst Bn. is ordered to occupy Fort Beersheba at earliest possible moment consistent with safety of the command and at the discretion of Bn. CO.
3. Immediate airborne assault on Fort Beersheba is authorized, provided that assault risks no more than 10% of effective strength of 501st Bn.
4. Any assault on Fort Beersheba in advance of main body of 501st Bn. shall be commanded by officer other than CO 501st Bn., and request of Captain Falkenberg to accompany assault and return to Bn. after Fort Beersheba is taken is expressly denied.

NOTE: It is the considered judgment of undersigned that officers assigned to 501st would not be competent to organize Bn. and accomplish main objective of pacification of Jordan Valley without supervision of experienced officer. It is further considered judgment of undersigned that secondary objective of early capture of Fort Beersheba does not justify endangering main mission of occupation of Jordan Valley. Captain Falkenberg is therefore ordered to refrain from exposing himself to combat risks until such time as primary mission is assured.

By Order of Planetary Military Commander

Nicholas Harrington, Colonel, CoDominium Marines

"Lazar, I take it you were listening to our conversation earlier," I said.

"No way to avoid it, sir. The lady was shouting." Lazar's expression didn't change.

I turned the book over and over in my hands. "Sergeant Major."

"Sir."

"I'm finished with this order book. Would you please see that it's returned to the battalion safe? Also, I think I forgot to log it out. You may do as you see fit about that."

"Sir."

"Thank you. You and Lazar may go now. I see no reason why the captain should be disturbed because I wanted a look at the order book."

"Yes, sir. Let's go, Monitor." Ogilvie started to say something else, but he stopped himself. They left, closing the door behind them.

"That was nice of you," Kathryn said.

"About all I could do," I said. "Would you like a drink?"

"No, thank you. I feel like a fool—"

"You're not the only one. I was just thinking the same thing, and for about the same reasons, when Ogilvie knocked. Won't you sit down? I suppose we should open the door."

"Don't be silly." She pulled a chair up to the big table. She was wearing a long plaid skirt, like a very long kilt, with a shiny blouse of some local fabric, and a wool jacket that didn't close at the front. Her hair was long, brown with red in it, but I thought it might be a wig. A damned pretty girl, I thought. But there was that haunted look in her eyes, and her hands were scarred, tiny scars that showed regeneration therapy by unskilled surgeons.

"I think Irina said you're a farmer. You don't look like a farmer."

She didn't smile. "I own a farm . . . or did. It's been confiscated by the government—one of our governments." Her voice was bitter. "The Mission Hills Protective Association. A gang of convicts. We used to fight them. My grandfather and my mother and my brother and my fiancé were all killed fighting them. Now we don't do anything at all."

"How many of these gangsters are there?"

She shrugged. "I guess the Protectionists have about four thousand. Something like that, anyway. Then there is the True Brotherhood. They have only a few hundred, maybe a thousand. No one really knows. They aren't really very well organized."

"Seems like they'd be no problem."

"They wouldn't be, if we could deal with them, but the Protective Association keeps our farmers disarmed and won't let us go on commando against the Brotherhood. They're afraid we'll throw the Association out, as well. The Brotherhood isn't anything real—they're closer to savages than human beings—but we can't do anything about them because the Association won't let us."

"And how many of you are there?"

"There are twenty thousand farmers in the Valley," she said. "And don't tell me we ought to be able to run both gangs off. I know we should be able to. But we tried it, and it didn't work. Whenever they raided one of our places, we'd turn out to chase them down, but they'd run into the hills, where it would take weeks to find them. Then they'd wait until we came down to grow crops again, then come down and kill everyone who resisted them, families and all."

"Is that what happened to your grandfather?"

"Yes. He'd been one of the Valley leaders. They weren't really trying to loot his place; they just wanted to kill him. I tried to organize resistance after that, and then—" She looked at her hands. "They caught me. I guess I will have that drink, after all."

"There's only brandy, I'm afraid. Or coffee."

"Brandy is all right."

I got another glass and poured. Her hands didn't shake as she lifted it.

"Aren't you going to ask?" she said. "Everyone wants to know, but they're afraid to ask." She shuddered. "They don't want to embarrass me. Embarrass!"

"Look, you don't want to talk about—"

"I don't want to, but I have to. Can you understand that?"

"Yes."

"Hal, there's very little you can imagine that they didn't do to me. The only reason I lived through it was that they wanted me to live. Afterward, they put me in a cage in the village square. As an example. A warning."

"I'd have thought that would have the opposite effect." I was trying to speak calmly, but inside I was boiling with hatred.

"No. I wish it had. It would have been worth it. Maybe—I don't know. The second night I was there, two men who'd been neighbors killed one of their guards and got me out. The Protectionists shot thirty people the next day in reprisal." She looked down at her hands. "My friends got me to a safe place. The doctor wasn't very well trained, they tell me. He left scars. If they could see what I was like when I got to him, they wouldn't say that."

I didn't know what to say. I didn't trust myself to say anything. I wanted to take her in my arms and hold her, not anything else, just hold her and protect her. And I wanted to get my hands on the people who'd done this, and on anyone who could have stopped it and didn't. My God, what are soldiers for, if not to put a stop to things like that? But all I could do was pour her another drink. I tried to keep my voice calm. "What will you do now?"

"I don't know. When Father Reedy finally let me leave his place, I went to Harmony. I guess I hoped I could get help. But . . . Hal, why won't Governor Swale do something? Anything?"

"More a matter of why should he," I said. "God, Kathryn, how can I say it? From his view, things are quiet. He can report that all's well here. They don't promote troublemakers in BuColonial, and Hugo Swale doesn't strike me as the kind of man who wants to retire on Arrarat." I drained my brandy glass. "Maybe I'm not being fair to him. Somehow I don't even want to be."

"But you'd help us if you could. Wouldn't you?"

"My God, yes. At least you're safe now."

She had a sad little smile. "Yes, nothing but a few scars. Come here. Please." She stood. I went to her. "Put your hands on my shoulders," she said.

I reached out to her. She stood rigidly. I could feel her trembling as I touched her.

"It happens every time," she said. "Even now, and I like you. I . . . Hal, I'd give anything if I could just relax and let you hold me. But I can't. It's all I can do to sit here and talk to you."

"Then I'd better let you go."

"No. Please. Please understand. I like you. I want to talk with you. I want to show myself there are men I can trust. Just . . . don't expect too much . . . not for a while. I keep telling myself I'm going to get over it. I don't want to be alone, but I'm afraid to be with anyone, and I'm going to get over that."

TEN

We had more weeks of parades and training. Falkenberg had a new scheme. He bought two hundred mules and assigned my company the job of learning to live with them. The idea was to increase our marching capability by using pack mules, and to teach the men to hang on to the pack saddles so they could cover more kilometers each day. It worked fine, but it only increased the frustration because there was nothing to march toward.

Governor Swale had gone back to Garrison, but Irina and Kathryn stayed as guests of the battalion. The men were pleased to have them on the post, and there was much less of a problem with discipline. They particularly adopted Kathryn. She was interested in everything they did, and the troops thought of her as a mascot. She was young and vulnerable, and she didn't talk down to them, and they were half in love with her.

I was more than that. I saw so much of her that Falkenberg thought it worthwhile to remind me that the service does not permit lieutenants to marry.

That isn't strictly true, of course, but it might as well be. There's no travel allowance and it takes an appeal to Saint Peter or perhaps an even higher level to get married quarters. The rule is, "Captains may marry, Majors should marry, Colonels must marry," and there aren't many exceptions to it.

"Not much danger of that," I told him.

"Yes?" He raised an eyebrow. It was an infuriating gesture.

I blurted out her story.

He only nodded. "I was aware of most of it, Mr. Slater."

"How in God's name can you be so cool about it?" I demanded. "I know you don't like her after that outburst—"

"Miss Malcolm has been very careful to apologize and to credit you with the explanation," Falkenberg said. "And the next time you take the order book out of the safe, I'll expect you to log it properly. Now tell me why we have three men of your company sleeping under their bunks without blankets."

He didn't really want an explanation, of course, and for that matter he probably already knew. There wasn't much about the battalion that he didn't know. It made a smooth change of subject, but I wasn't having any. I told him, off the record, what the charges would have been if I'd officially heard what the men had done. "Centurion Ardwain preferred not to report it," I said. "Captain, I still cannot understand how you can be so calm when you know that not two hundred kilometers from here—"

"Mr. Slater, I remain calm because at the moment there is very little I can do. What do you want? That we lead the 501st in a mutiny? If it is any comfort to you, I do not think the situation will last. It is my belief that Governor Swale is living in a fool's paradise. You cannot deal with criminal gangs on any permanent basis, and I believe the situation will explode. Until it does, there is not one damned thing we can do, and I prefer not to be reminded of my helplessness."

"But, sir—"

"But nothing, Mr. Slater. Shut up and soldier."

Falkenberg had guessed right. Although we didn't know it, about the time we had that conversation the Protective Association had decided to raise the price of grain. Two weeks later they hiked the price again and held up the shipments to show the Governor they meant it.

It wasn't long after that the Governor paid another visit to Fort Beersheba.

Deane Knowles found me in the club. "His Excellency has arrived," he said. "He's really come with full kit this time. He's brought Colonel Harrington and a whole company of militia."

"What the devil are they for?" I asked.

"Search me."

"I thought you knew everything, well, well. I suppose we will know soon enough. There's Officers' Call."

The Governor, Colonel Harrington, and Falkenberg were all in the staff conference room. There was also a colonel of militia. He didn't look very soldierly. His uniform was baggy, and he had a bulge around his middle. The Governor introduced him as Colonel Trevor.

"I'll come right to the point, gentlemen," Swale said. "Due to certain developments in the southern areas, I am no longer confident that food supply for the cities of Harmony and Garrison is assured. The local government down there has not negotiated in good faith. It's time to put some pressure on them."

"In other words," Colonel Harrington said, "he

wants to send the Marines down to bash heads so the Harmony merchants won't have to pay so much."

"Colonel, that remark was not called for," Governor Swale said.

"Certainly it was." There was no humor in Harrington's voice. "If we can send my lads down to get themselves killed, we can tell them why they're going. It's hardly a new mission for the Line Marines."

"Your orders are to hold the cities," Swale said. "That cannot be done without adequate food supplies. I think that justifies using your troops for this campaign."

"Sure it does," Harrington said. "And after the CD pulls both of us out of here, what happens? Doesn't that worry you a bit, Colonel Trevor?"

"The CoDominium won't abandon Arrarat." Trevor sounded very positive.

"You're betting a lot on that," Colonel Harrington told him.

"If you two are quite through," Swale said. "Captain, how soon can your battalion be ready to march?"

Falkenberg looked to Colonel Harrington. "Are we to hold the Jordan area, as well, sir?"

"You won't need much here," Harrington said. "The militia can take over now."

"And what precisely are we to accomplish in the southern farm area?" Falkenberg asked.

"I just told you," Swale said. "Go down and put some pressure on the Protective Association so they'll see reason."

"And how am I to do that?"

"For heaven's sake, Falkenberg, it's a punitive expedition. Go hurt them until they're ready to give in."

"Burn farms and towns. Shoot livestock. Destroy transport systems. That sort of thing?"

"Well . . . I'd rather you didn't do it that way."

"Then, Governor, exactly what am I to do?" Falkenberg demanded. "I remind you that the Protective Association is itself an occupying power. They don't really care what we do to the farmers. They don't work that land; they merely expropriate from those who do."

"Then confine your punitive actions to the Protective Association—" Swale's voice trailed off.

"I do not even know how to identify them, sir. I presume that anyone I find actually working the land is probably not one of the criminal element, but I can hardly shoot everyone who happens to be idle at the moment I pass through."

"You needn't be sarcastic with me, *Captain*."

"Sir, I am trying to point out the difficulties inherent in the orders you gave me. If I have been impertinent, you have my apology."

Sure you do, I thought. Deane and Louis grinned at each other and at me. Then we managed to get our faces straight. I wondered what Falkenberg was trying to do. I found out soon enough.

"Then what the devil do you suggest?" Swale demanded.

"Governor, there is a way I can assure you a reasonable and adequate grain supply. It requires your cooperation. Specifically, you must withdraw recognition from the Protective Association."

"And recognize whom? An unorganized bunch of farmers who couldn't hold on to the territory in the first place? Captain, I have sympathy for those people, even if all of you here do suspect me of being a monster with no feelings. My sympathy is of no matter. I must feed the people of Harmony, and to do that I'll deal with the devil himself if that's what it takes."

"And you very nearly have," I muttered.

"What's that, Lieutenant Slater?"

"Nothing, Governor. Excuse me."

"I expect I know what you said. Captain, let's suppose I do what you ask and withdraw recognition from the Protective Association. Now what do I do? We are not in the democracy-building business. My personal sympathies may well lie with what we are pleased to call 'free and democratic institutions,' but I happen to be an official of the CoDominium, not of the United States. So, by the way, do you. If this planet had been settled by Soviets, we wouldn't even be having this conversation. There would be an assured grain supply, and no nonsense about it."

"I hardly think the situations are comparable," Colonel Harrington said.

"Nor I," Trevor added. That surprised me.

"I ask again, what do we do?" the Governor said.

"Extend CoDominium protection to the area," Harrington said. "It needn't be permanent. I make no doubt that Colonel Trevor's people have friends among the farmers. We may not be in the democracy-building business, but there are plenty who'd like to try."

"You are asking for all-out war on the Protective Association," Swale said. "Colonel Harrington, have you any idea of what that will cost? The Senate is very reluctantly paying the basic costs of keeping these Marines on Arrarat. They have not sent one deci-credit to pay for combat actions. How am I supposed to *pay* for this war?"

"You'll just have to tax the grain transactions, that's all," Harrington said.

"I can't do that."

"You're going to have to do it. Captain Falkenberg is right. We can drive out the Protective Association— with enough local cooperation—but we sure as hell can't grow wheat for you. I suppose we could exterminate everyone in the whole damned valley and repopulate it—"

"Now *you're* being impertinent."

"My apologies," Harrington said. "Governor, just what *do* you want? Those farmers aren't going to grow crops just to have a bunch of gangsters take the profits. They'll move out first, or take the land out of cultivation. Then what happens to your grain supply?"

"The situation is more complex than you think, Colonel. Believe me, it is. Your business is war and violence. Mine is politics, and I tell you that things aren't always what they seem. The Protective Association can keep Harmony supplied with grain at a reasonable price. That's what we must have, and it's what you're going to get for me. Now you tell me that my only alternatives are a war I can't pay for, or starvation in the city. Neither is acceptable. I order you to send an expeditionary force to Allansport. It will have the limited objective of demonstrating our intent and putting sufficient pressure on the Protective Association to make them reasonable, and that is the whole objective."

Harrington studied his fingernails for a moment. "Sir, I cannot accept the responsibility."

"Damn you. Captain Falkenberg, you will—"

"I can't accept the responsibility, either, Governor."

"Then, by God, I'll have Colonel Trevor lead it. Trevor, if you say you can't accept responsibility, I damned well know a dozen militia officers who can."

"Yes, sir. Who'll command the Marines sir? They won't take orders from me. Not directly."

"The lieutenants will—" He stopped, because one by one, Deane, Louis, and I all shook our heads.

"This is blackmail! I'll have every one of you cashiered!"

Colonel Harrington laughed. "Now, you know, I really doubt that. Me you might manage to get at.

But junior officers for refusing an assignment their colonel turned down? Try peddling that to Admiral Lermontov and he'll laugh like hell."

Swale sat down. He struggled for a moment until he was in control of his voice. "Why are you doing this?"

Colonel Harrington shook his head slowly. "Governor, everything you said about the service is true. We're used. They use us to bash heads so that some senator's nephew can make a mega-credit. They hand people a raw deal and then call on us to make the victims stay in the game. Most of the time we have to take it. It doesn't mean we like it much. Once in a while, just every now and then, the Fleet gets a chance to put something right after you civilians mess it up. We don't pass up such chances." Harrington's voice had been quiet, but now he let it rise slightly. "Governor, just what the hell do you think men become soldiers for? So that you can get promoted to a cushy job?"

"I have told you, I would like to help those farmers. I can't do it. Cannot you understand? We can't *pay* for a long campaign. *Can't.* Not won't. Can't."

"Yes, sir," Colonel Harrington said. "I expect I'd better get back to Garrison. The staff's going to have to work out a pretty strict rationing plan."

"You think you have won," the Governor said. "Not yet, Colonel. Not yet. Colonel Trevor, I asked you to put a battalion of militia on riverboats. How long will it take for them to get here?"

"Be here tomorrow, sir."

"When they arrive, I want you to have made arrangements for more fuel and supplies. We are taking that battalion to Allansport, where I will personally direct operations. I've no doubt we can make the Protective Association see reason. As to the rest of you, you will sit in this fort and rot for all I care. Good afternoon, gentlemen."

I told Kathryn about the conference when I met her for supper that night. She listened with bewilderment.

"I don't understand, Hal," she finally blurted. "All that fuss about costs. *We'd* pay for the campaign and be happy to do it."

"Do you think the Governor knows that?" I asked.

"Of course he knows it. I've told him, and I've brought him offers from some of the other farmers. Don't you remember I asked him to loan us the 501st?"

"Sure, but you weren't serious."

"I wasn't then, but it sounded like such a good idea that later on we really tried to hire you. He wasn't interested."

"Wasn't interested in what?" Louis Bonneyman asked. "Is this an intimate conversation, or may I join you?"

"Please do," Kathryn said. "We're just finishing—"

"I've had my dinner, also," Louis said. "But I'll buy you a drink. Hal, did you ever think old Harrington had that kind of guts?"

"No. Surprised me. So what happens next?"

"Beats me," Louis said. "But I'll give you a hint. I just finished helping Sergeant Major cut orders putting this whole outfit on full field alert as of reveille tomorrow."

"Figures. I wonder just how much trouble His Excellency will get himself into."

Louis grinned. "With any luck, he'll get himself killed and Colonel Harrington becomes Acting Governor. Then we can really clean house."

"You can't wish that on Irina's father," Kathryn protested. "I thought you liked her, Louis."

"Her, yes. Her old man I can live without. I'd have thought you'd share the sentiment."

"He was kind enough to let me live in his home," Kathryn said. "I don't understand him at all. He seems like a good man. It's only when—"

"When he puts on his Governor's hat," I said. "I keep wondering if we blew it, Kathryn. If we'd taken the Governor up on his offer, we could at least have gotten down there to do *something*. I might even have caught the bastard that— You know who I mean."

"I'm glad you didn't, Hal. It would have been horrible. Anything you did to those gangsters they'd take out on my friends as soon as you'd left. I wouldn't have helped you, and I don't think anyone else would, because anybody that did would be signing death warrants for his whole family, and all his friends, too."

"Sounds like a rough gang," Louis said. "Thorough. If you're going to use terror, go all the way. Unfortunately, it works."

Kathryn nodded. "Yes. I've tried to explain it to Governor Swale. If he sends an expedition there, a lot of my friends will try to help. They'll be killed if he leaves those hoodlums in control when it's over. It would be better if none of you ever went there."

"But the Harmony merchants don't like the prices," Louis said. "They want their grain cheaper, and Swale's got to worry about them, too. A complaint from the Harmony city council wouldn't look too good on his record. Somebody at BuColonial might take it seriously."

"Politics," Kathryn said. "Why can't—"

"Be your age," Louis said. "There's politics in the CoDominium, sure, but we still keep the peace. And it's not all that bad, anyway. Swale was appointed by Grand Senator Bronson's people."

"An unsavory lot," I said.

"Maybe," Louis admitted. "Anyway, of course that means that Bronson's enemies will be looking for reasons to discredit Swale. He's got to be careful. The Harmony merchants still have friends at American Express—and AmEx hates Bronson with a passion."

"I'd say our Governor has problems, then," I said. "From the looks of the troops he took with him, he won't scare the Association much. The militia have pretty uniforms, but they're all city kids. All right for holding walls and cruising along the Jordan now that we've disarmed everybody here, but they're unlikely to scare anybody with real combat experience."

ELEVEN

We put the entire battalion on ready alert, but nothing happened for a week. Colonel Harrington stayed at Fort Beersheba and joined us in the officers' mess in the evenings. Like Falkenberg, he liked bagpipes. To my horror, so did Kathryn. I suppose every woman has some major failing.

"What the hell is he doing?" Colonel Harrington demanded. "I'd have sworn he'd have gotten himself into trouble by now. Maybe we've overestimated the Mission Hills Protective Association. Why the hell did they come up with that name? There aren't any Mission Hills on this planet, to the best of my knowledge."

"They brought the name with them, Colonel," Louis told him. "There's a Southern California gang with that name. Been around for two or three generations. A number of them happened to be on the same prison ship, and they stuck together when they got there."

"How the hell did you find that out?" Harrington demanded.

143

"Captain Falkenberg insists that his people be thorough," Louis said. "It was a matter of sifting through enough convicts until I found one who knew, and then finding some corroboration."

"Well, congratulations, Louis," Harrington said. "John, you've done well with your collection of newlies."

"Thank you, Colonel."

"Real test's coming up now, though. What the hell is happening down there? Steward, another whiskey, all around. If we can't fight, we can still drink."

"Maybe Governor Swale will come to terms with them," I said.

The colonel gave me a sour look. "Doubt it, Hal. He's between a rock and a hard place. The merchants won't stand for the prices those goons want, and they think they've got him by the balls. They're not afraid of us, you know. They've got a good idea of what's going on in Harmony. They know damned well that Fleet isn't sending any more support to Arrarat, and what the hell can a thousand men do? Even a thousand Line Marines?"

"I hope they think that way," Deane said. "If they'll stand and fight, they're finished—"

"But they won't," John Falkenberg said. "They're no fools. They won't stand and fight, they'll run like hell as soon as we get close to them. They've only to sit up in the hills and avoid us. Eventually we'll have to leave, but they won't."

Harrington nodded. "Yeah. In the long run those poor damned farmers will have to cut it for themselves. Maybe they'll make it. At least we can try to set things right for them. John, do you think the pipers have had their drink by now?"

"I'm certain of it, Colonel. Lazar! Have Pipe Major bring us a tune!"

* * *

Eight days after the Governor left Fort Beersheba, we still had no word. That night there was the usual drinking with the pipers in the mess. I excused myself early and went up to my rooms with Kathryn. I still couldn't touch her without setting her to trembling, but we were working on it. I'd decided I was in love with her, and I could wait for the physical aspects to develop. I didn't dare think very far ahead. We had no real future that I could see, but for the moment just being together was enough. It wasn't a situation either of us enjoyed, but we hated to be separated.

The phone buzzed. "Slater," I told it.

"Sergeant Major Ogilvie, sir. You're wanted in the staff room immediately."

"Hallelujah. Be right there, Sergeant Major." As I hung up, Brady's trumpet sounded "On Full Kits." I turned to Kathryn. We were both grinning like idiots. "This is it, sweetheart."

"Yes. Now that it's happened, I'm scared."

"So am I. As Falkenberg says, we're all scared, but it's an officer's job not to show it. Be back when I can—"

"Just a second." She came to me and put her hands on my shoulders. Her arms went around me, and she pulled me against herself. "See? I'm hardly shaking at all." She kissed me, quickly, then a long, lingering kiss.

"This is one hell of a time for a miraculous psychiatric cure," I said.

"Shut up and get out of here."

"Aye, aye, ma'am." I went out quickly.

Hartz was in the hallway. "I will have our gear ready, zur," he said. "And now we fight."

"I hope so."

As I walked across the parade ground, I wondered why I felt so good. We were about to go kill and maim a lot of people, and give them the chance to do it to us. For a million reasons we ought to have been afraid, and we ought to dread what was coming, but we didn't.

Is it that what we think we ought to do is so thoroughly alien to what we really feel? I couldn't kid myself that this time was different because our cause was just. We say we love peace, but it doesn't excite us. Even pacifists talk more about the horrors of war than about the glories of peace.

And you're not supposed to solve the problems of the universe, I told myself. But you do get to kill the man that raped your girl.

The others were already in the conference room, with Colonel Harrington at the head of the table.

"The expected has happened," Harrington said. I knew for a fact that he'd drunk four double whiskeys since supper, but there wasn't a trace of it in his speech. I'd swallowed two quick-sober pills on the way over. I really hadn't needed them. I was sure they hadn't had time to dissolve, but I felt fine.

"Our Governor has managed to get himself besieged in Allansport," Harrington said. "With half of his force outside the town. He wants us to bail him out. I have told him we will march immediately— for a price."

"Then he's agreed to withdraw recognition of the Association?" Deane asked.

"Agreed to, yes. He hasn't done it yet. I think he's afraid that the instant he does, they will get really nasty. However, I have his word on it, and I will hold him to it. Captain Falkenberg, the 501st is hereby ordered to drive the Mission Hills Protective Association out of the Allan River Valley by whatever means you think best. You may cooperate with local partisan forces in the area and make reasonable agreements with them. The entire valley is to be placed under CoDominium protection."

"Aye, aye, sir." Falkenberg's detached calm broke for a moment and he let a note of triumph get into his voice.

"Now, Captain, if you will be kind enough to review your battle plan," Harrington said.

"Sir." Falkenberg used the console to project a map onto the briefing screen.

I'd already memorized the area, but I examined it again. About ten kilometers upriver from Beersheba, the Jordan was joined by a tributary known as the Allan River. The Allan runs southwest through forest lands for about fifty kilometers, then turns and widens in a valley that lies almost due north-south. The east side of the Allan Valley is narrow, because no more than twenty klicks from the river there's a high mountain range and east of that is high desert. Nobody lives there and nobody would want to. The west side, though, is some of the most fertile land on Arrarat. The valley is irregularly shaped, narrowing to no more than twenty-five klicks wide in places, but opening out to more than one hundred klicks in others. It reminded me of the San Joaquin Valley of California, a big fertile bowl with rugged mountains on both sides of it.

Allansport is one hundred twenty-five klicks upriver from where the Allan runs into the Jordan. Falkenberg left the big valley map on one screen and projected a detail onto the other. He fiddled with the console to bring red and green lines representing friendly and hostile forces onto the map.

"As you can see, Governor Swale and one company of militia have taken a defensive position in Allansport," Falkenberg said. "The other two militia companies are south of him, actually upriver. How the devil he ever got himself into such a stupid situation, I cannot say."

"Natural talent," Colonel Harrington muttered.

"No doubt," Falkenberg said. "We have two objectives. The minor, but most urgent, is to rescue Governor Swale. The major objective is pacification of the area. It seems very unlikely that we can accomplish that without a general uprising of the locals in our favor. Agreed?"

We were all silent for a moment. "Mr. Bonneyman, I believe you're the junior," Colonel Harrington said.

"Agreed, sir," Louis said.

Deane and I spoke at once. "Agreed."

"Excellent. I remind you that this conference is recorded," Falkenberg said.

Of course, I thought. All staff conferences are. It didn't seem like Falkenberg and Harrington to spread responsibility around by getting our opinions on record, but I was sure they had their reasons.

"The best way to stimulate a general uprising would be to inflict an immediate and major defeat on the Protective Association," Falkenberg said. "A defeat, not merely driving them away, but bringing them to battle and eliminating a large number of them. It is my view that this is sufficiently important to justify considerable risks. Is that agreed to?"

Aha! I thought. Starting with Louis, we all stated our agreements.

"Then we can proceed to the battle plan," Falkenberg said. "It is complex, but I think it is worth a try. You will notice that there is a pass into the hills west of Allansport. Our informants tell us that this is the route the Association forces will take if they are forced to retreat. Furthermore, there is a sizable militia force south of Allansport. If the militia were strengthened with local partisans, and if we can take the pass before the besieging hostiles realize their danger, we will have them trapped. The main body of the battalion will march upriver, approach from the north, and engage them. We won't get them all, but we should be able to eliminate quite a lot of them. With that kind of victory behind us, persuading the other ranchers to rise up and join us should not be difficult."

As he talked he illustrated the battle plan with lights on the map. He was right. It was complex.

"Questions?" Falkenberg asked.

"Sir," I said, "I don't believe those two militia companies can take the pass. I certainly wouldn't count on it."

"They can't," Harrington said. "But they're pretty steady on defense. Give 'em a strong position to hold and those lads will give a good account of themselves."

"Yes," Falkenberg said. "I propose to stiffen the militia outside the city with two sections of Marines. We still have our Skyhooks, and I see no reason why we can't use them again."

"Here we go again," I muttered. "Even so, sir, it all depends on how strongly that pass is held, and we don't know that. Or do we?"

"Only that it will be defended," Falkenberg said. "The attack on the pass will have to be in the nature of a probe, ready to be withdrawn if the opposition is too stiff."

"I see." I thought about that for a while. I'd never done anything like that, of course. I might have a military medal, but I couldn't kid myself about my combat experience. "I think I can manage that, sir," I said.

Falkenberg gave me his half grin, the expression

he used when he was springing one of his surprises. "I'm afraid you won't have all the fun this time, Mr. Slater. I intend to lead the Skyhook force myself. You'll have command of the main body."

There was more to his plan, including a part I didn't like at all. He was taking Kathryn with him on the Skyhook. I couldn't really object. She'd already volunteered. Falkenberg had called her in my rooms while I was on the way over to the conference.

"I really have little choice," Falkenberg said. "We must have someone reliable who is known to the locals. The whole plan depends or getting enough local assistance to seal off the valley to the south of Allansport. Otherwise, there's no point to it."

I had to agree. I didn't have to like it. I could imagine what she'd say if I tried to stop her.

Falkenberg finished with the briefing. "Any more questions? No? Then once again I'll ask for your opinions."

"Looks all right to me," Louis said. Of course he would. He was going with Falkenberg in the Skyhooks.

"No problem with heavy weapons," Deane said. "I like it."

"Mr. Slater?"

"My operation looks straightforward enough. No problems."

"It's straightforward," Colonel Harrington said, "but not trivial. You've got the trickiest part of the job. You have to seal off the northern escape route, engage the enemy, rescue the Governor, and then swing around like a hammer to smash the hostiles against the anvil Captain Falkenberg will erect at the passes. The timing is critical."

"I have confidence in Lieutenant Slater," Falkenberg said.

"So have I, or I wouldn't approve this plan,"

Harrington said. "But don't ignore what we're doing here. In order to carry out the major objective of clearing the hostiles from the whole valley, we're leaving Governor Swale in a rather delicate situation. If something goes wrong, Sector will have our heads—with justice, I might add." He stood, and we all got to our feet. "But I like it. No doubt the Association thinks we'll be rushing directly to the Governor's aid, and their people are prepared for that. I hate to be obvious."

"So do I," Falkenberg said.

Harrington nodded curtly. "Gentlemen, you have your orders."

The riverboats looked like something out of the American Civil War as they puffed their way down the dark river. We'd had a rainstorm when we left the fort, but now the sky was clear and dark, with bright stars overhead. My rivercraft were really nothing more than barges with steam engines and enough superstructure to get cargo under cover. They were made of wood, of course; there wasn't enough of a metals industry on Arrarat to build steel hulls, and not much reason to want to.

I had three barges, each about fifty meters long and twenty wide, big rectangular floating platforms with cabins whose roofs served as raised decks, and a central bridge to control them. Every centimeter of available space was covered with troops, mules, guns, supply wagons, ammunition, tentage, and rations. The 501st was going to the Allan Valley to stay.

The barges burned wood, which we had to stop and cut with chain saws. In addition, I had one amphibious hovercraft with light armor. It could make fifty-five kilometers an hour compared to the eleven kilometers an hour the barges got under full steam.

Perched on top of the third barge was Number Three helicopter, which could make a couple of hundred kilometers an hour. The discrepancies in speeds would have been amusing if they weren't so frustrating.

"One goddamned DC-45," Deane said. "One. That's all, one Starlifter, and we could be there in an hour."

"We make do with what we got," I told him. "Besides, think how romantic it all is. Pity we don't have a leadsman up in the bows singing out the river depth, instead of a sonar depth finder."

The hovercraft ran interference to be sure there weren't any nasty surprises waiting for us. As we got closer to Allansport, I sent up the chopper to make a high-altitude survey of the landing area. We were landing a good twenty klicks downriver from Allansport. Not only were the banks a lot steeper farther upriver, but we didn't want to scare the Association off by landing too close. Governor Swale was screaming at me hourly, of course. He wanted us in Allansport right now. When I told him where we were putting ashore, he was almost hysterical.

"What the hell are you doing?" he demanded. "All you have to do is show up! They won't stand and fight you. This is all a political maneuver. Put heavy pressure on them and they'll come to terms."

I didn't point out that we didn't intend to come to terms with the Association. "Sir, Colonel Harrington approved the battle plan."

"I don't care if God the Father approved it!" Swale shouted. "What are you doing? I know Falkenberg is south of here with troops he brought in by helicopter, but he won't tell me what he's doing! And now he's withdrawn the militia! I'm trapped in here, and you're playing some kind of game! I demand to know what you intend!"

"Governor, I don't know myself," I said. "I just

know what my orders are. We'll have you out of there in a few hours. Out." I switched off the set and turned to Deane.

"Well," I said, "we know Louis and Falkenberg are doing something down south of us. Wish I knew how they're making out."

"If there's something we need to know, they'll tell us," Deane said. "Worried about Kathryn?"

"Some."

"Never get so attached to anyone that you worry about her. Saves a lot of skull sweat."

"Yeah, sure. Helmsman, that looks like our landing area. Look sharp."

"Aye, aye, sir."

"Hartz, get me the chopper pilot."

"Zur." Hartz fiddled with the radio for a moment, then handed me the mike.

"Sergeant Stragoff, sir."

"Stragoff, I want you to make a complete sweep of our landing area. There should be two unarmed people there to meet us. They'll show you a blue light. If they show any other color, spray the whole area and get the hell out of there. If they show blue, tell me about it, but I still want a complete survey."

"Aye, aye, sir."

"And just who is meeting us?" Deane asked.

"Don't know their names," I said. "Falkenberg said he'd try to set up a welcoming committee of local resistance types. If we're satisfied with them, we help 'em arm some of their neighbors. That's why we brought those extra rifles."

The radio came to life again. "Two people with a blue light, sir. Nothing else on radar or IR."

"Good. Okay, now make a wider sweep. I don't want to find out there's an artillery battery registered on our landing area."

"Sir."

"Sergeant Major," I said.

"Sir."

"You can take the hovercraft in to occupy the landing area. Treat the welcoming committee politely, but keep an eye on them. When the area's secure, we'll all go ashore."

"Sir."

I looked up at the stars. There was no moon. About five hours to dawn. With any luck we'd be deployed and ready for combat by first light. "Okay, Deane, you're in charge," I said. "Hartz, you stay with him."

"If the lieutenant orders it."

"Damn it, I did order it. Belay that. All right, come with me."

We went to the deck level. The river was less than a meter below us. It wasn't a river to swim in; there are aquatic snakes on Arrarat, and their poison will finish off anything that has protein in it. It acts as a catalyst to coagulate cell bodies. I had no real desire to be a hard rubber lump.

We had one canoe on board. I'd already found troopers who knew something about handling them. We had a dozen men familiar with the screwy watercraft, which didn't surprise me. The story is that you can find *any* skill in a Line Marine regiment, and it seems to be true. In my own company I had two master masons, an artist, a couple of electronic techs (possibly engineers, but they weren't saying), at least one disbarred lawyer, a drunken psychiatrist, and a chap the men claimed was a defrocked preacher.

Corporal Anuraro showed me how to get into the canoe without swamping it. We don't have those things in Arizona. As they paddled me ashore, I thought about how silly the situation was. I was being paddled in a canoe, a device invented at least ten thousand years ago. I was carrying a pair of light-amplifying field glasses based on a principle not discovered until after I was born. Behind me was a steamboat that might have been moving up the Missouri River at the time of Custer's last stand, and I got to this planet in a starship.

The current was swift, and I was glad to have experienced men at the paddles. The water flowed smoothly alongside. Sometimes an unseen creature made riffles in it. Over on the shore the hovercraft had already landed, and someone was signaling us with a light. When we got to the bank I was glad to be on dry land.

"Where are our visitors, Roszak?" I asked.

"Over here, sir."

Two men, both ranchers or farmers. One was Oriental. They looked to be about fifty years old. As agreed, they weren't armed.

"I'm Lieutenant Slater," I said.

The Oriental answered. "I am Wan Loo. This is Harry Seeton."

"I've heard of you. Kathryn says you helped her, once."

"Yes. To escape from a cage," Wan Loo said.

"You're supposed to prove something," I said.

Wan Loo smiled softly. "You have a scar on your left arm. It is shaped like a scimitar. When you were a boy you had a favorite horse named Candybar."

"You've seen Kathryn," I said. "Where is she?"

"South of Allansport. She is trying to raise a force of ranchers to reinforce Captain Falkenberg. We were sent here to assist you."

"We've done pretty well," Harry Seeton added. "A lot of ranchers will fight if you can furnish weapons. But there's something else."

"Yes?"

"Please do not think we are not grateful," Wan

Loo said. "But you must understand. We have fought for years, and we cannot fight any longer. We have an uneasy peace in this valley. It is the peace of submission, and we do not care for it, but we will not throw it away simply to help you. If you have not come to stay, please take your soldiers, rescue your Governor, and go away without involving us."

"That's blunt enough," I said.

"We have to be blunt," Harry Seeton said. "Wan Loo isn't talking for us. We're outlaws, anyway. We're with you no matter what happens. But we can't go ask our friends to join if you people don't mean it when you say you'll stay and protect them."

"It is an old story," Wan Loo said. "You cannot blame the farmers. They would rather have you than the Association, but if you are here only for a little while, and the Association is here forever, what can they do? My ancestors were faced with the same problem on Earth. They chose to support the West, and when the Americans, who had little stake in the war, withdrew their forces, my great-grandfather gave up land his family had held for a thousand years to go with them. He had no choice. Do you think he would have chosen the American side if he had known that would happen?"

"The CoDominium has extended protection to this valley," I said.

"Governments have no honor," Wan Loo said. "Many people have none, either, but at least it is possible for a man to have honor. It is not possible for a government. Do you pledge that *you* will not abandon our friends if we arouse them for you?"

"Yes."

"Then we have your word. Kathryn says you are an honorable man. If you will help us with transportation and radio, by noon tomorrow I believe we will have five hundred people to assist you."

"And God help 'em if we lose," Seeton said. "God help 'em."

"We won't lose," I said.

"A battle is not a war," Wan Loo said. "And wars are not won by weapons, but by the will to win them. We will go now."

TWELVE

It is a basic military maxim that no battle plan ever survives contact with the enemy, but by noon it looked as if this operation would be an exception. Falkenberg's combat team—two platoons of B Company, brought down by Skyhook after we were aboard our barges—struck at the passes just before dawn and in three hours of sharp fighting had taken them over. He brought up two companies of militia to dig in and hold them.

Meanwhile, the ranchers in the south were armed and turned out on commando to block any southward retreat. I had only scattered reports from that sector, but all seemed under control. Kathryn had raised a force of nearly five hundred, which ought to be enough to hold the southern defensive line.

Then it was my turn. Two hours after dawn I had a skirmish line stretching eight kilometers into the valley. My left flank was anchored on the river. There'd be no problem there. The right flank was a different story.

"It bothers me," I told Falkenberg when I reported by radio. "My right flank is hanging in thin air. The only thing protecting us is Wan Loo's ranchers, and there's no more than three hundred of them—if that many." Wan Loo hadn't been as successful as Kathryn had been. Of course, he'd had a lot less time.

"And just what do you expect to hit you in the flank?" Falkenberg asked.

"I don't know. I just don't like it when we have to depend on other people—and on the enemy doing what we want them to do."

"Neither do I, but do you have an alternative to suggest?"

"No, sir."

"Then carry out your orders, Mr. Slater. Advance on Allansport."

"Aye, aye, sir."

It wasn't an easy battle line to control. I had units strung all across the valley, with the major strength on the left wing that advanced along the river. The terrain was open, gently rolling hills with lines of hedges and eucalyptus trees planted as windbreaks. The fields were recently harvested, and swine had been turned loose in the wheat stubble. The fields were muddy, but spread as we were, we didn't churn them up much.

The farmhouses were scattered at wide intervals. These had been huge farm holdings. The smallest were over a kilometer square, and some were much larger. A lot of the land was unworked. The houses were stone and earth, partly underground, built like miniature fortresses. Some had sections of wall blown out by explosives.

Harry Seeton was with me in my ground-effects caravan. When we came to a farmhouse, he'd try to persuade the owner and his children and relatives to join us. If they agreed, he'd send them off to join the growing number on our right wing.

"Something bothers me," I told Seeton. "Sure, you have big families and everybody works, but how did you cultivate all this land? That last place was at least five hundred hectares."

"Rainfall here's tricky," Seeton said. "Half the time we've got swamp, and the other half we have drought. The only fertilizer is manure. We've got to leave a lot of the land fallow, or planted in legumes to be plowed under."

"It still seems like a lot of work for just one family."

"Well, we had hired help. Convicts, mostly. Ungrateful bastards joined the Association gangs first chance they got. Tell me something, Lieutenant."

"Yes?"

"Are your men afraid they'll starve to death? I never saw anything like it, the way they pick up anything they can find." He pointed to one B Company trooper who was just ahead of us. He wasn't a large man to begin with, and he had his pockets stuffed with at least three chickens, several ears of corn, and a bottle he'd liberated somewhere. There were bulges in his pack that couldn't have come from regulation equipment, and he'd even strapped firewood on top of it so that we couldn't see his helmet from behind him. "They're like a plague of locusts," Seeton said.

"Not much I can do about it," I said. "I can't be everywhere, and the Line Marines figure anything that's not actually penned up and watched is fair game. They'll eat well for a few days—it beats monkey and greasy rice." I didn't add that if he thought things were bad now, with the troops on the way to a battle, he'd really be horrified after the troops had been in the field a few weeks.

There were shots from ahead. "It's started," I said.

"How many of these farm areas are still inhabited by your people?"

"Not many, this close to Allansport. The town itself is almost all Association people. Or goddamned collaborators, which is the same thing. I expect that's why they haven't blasted it down. They outnumber your Governor's escort by quite a lot."

"Yeah." That bothered me. Why hadn't the Association forces simply walked in and taken Governor Swale? As Seeton said, Swale had only a couple of companies of militia with him, yet the siege had been a stalemate. As if they hadn't really wanted to capture him.

Of course, they had problems no matter what they did. If they killed the Governor, Colonel Harrington would be in control. I had to assume the Protective Association had friends in Harmony, possibly even inside the palace. Certainly there were plenty of leaks. They'd know that Harrington was a tougher nut than Swale.

The resistance was stronger as we approached Allansport. The Association forces were far better armed than we'd expected them to be. They had mortars and light artillery, and plenty of ammunition for both.

We had two close calls with the helicopters. I'd sent them forward as gunships to support the advancing infantry. We found out the Association had target-seeking missiles, and the only reason they didn't get the choppers was that their gunners were too eager. They fired while the helicopters still had time to maneuver. I pulled the choppers back to headquarters. I could use them for reconnaissance, but I wasn't going to risk them in combat.

We silenced their artillery batteries one by one. They had plenty of guns, but their electronics were ineffective. Their counterbattery fire was pathetic.

We'd have a couple of exchanges, our radars would backtrack their guns, and that would be the end of it.

"Where the hell did they get all that stuff?" I asked Seeton.

"They've always had a lot of equipment. Since the first time they came out of the hills, they've been pretty well armed. Lately it's gotten a lot worse. One reason we gave up."

"It had to come from off-planet," I said. "How?"

"I don't know. Ask your governor."

"I intend to. That stuff had to come through the spaceport. Somebody's getting rich selling guns to the Protective Association."

We moved up to the outer fringes of Allansport. The town was spread across low hills next to the river. It had a protective wall made of brick and adobe, like the houses. Deane's artillery tore huge gaps in the wall and the troops moved into the streets beyond. The fighting was fierce. Seeton was right about the sentiments of the townspeople. They fought from house to house, and the Marines had to move cautiously, with plenty of artillery support. We were flattening the town as we moved into it.

Governor Swale and two companies of Harmony militia were dug in on the bluffs overlooking the river, very nearly in the center of the semicircular town. They held the riverfront almost to the steel bridge that crossed the Allan. I'd hoped to reach the Governor by dark, but the fighting in the town was too severe. At dusk I called to report that I wouldn't reach him for another day.

"However, we're within artillery range of your position," I told him. "We can give you fire support if there's any serious attempt to take your position by storm."

"Yes. You've done well," he told me.

That was a surprise. I'd expected him to read me

off for not getting there sooner. Live and learn, I told myself. "I'm bringing the right flank around in an envelopment," I told Swale. "By morning we'll have every one of them penned in Allansport, and we can deal with them at our leisure."

"Excellent," Swale said. "My militia officers tell me the Association forces have very little strength in the southern part of the town. You may be able to take many of the streets during the night."

We halted at dark. I sent Ardwain forward with orders to take A Company around the edges of the town and occupy sections at the southern end. Then I had supper with the troops. As Seeton had noticed, they'd provisioned themselves pretty well. No monkey and rice tonight! We had roast chicken and fresh corn.

After dark I went back to my map table. I'd parked the caravan next to a stone farmhouse two klicks from the outskirts of Allansport. Headquarters platoon set up the C.P., and there were a million details to attend to: supply, field hospitals, plans to evacuate wounded by helicopter, shuffling ammunition around to make sure each unit had enough of the right kind. The computers could handle a lot of it, but there were decisions to be made and no one to make them but me. Finally I had time to set up our positions into the map table computer and make new plans. By feeding the computer the proper inputs, it would show the units on the map, fight battles and display the probable outcomes, move units around under fire and subtract out casualties. . . .

It reminded me of the afternoon's battles. There'd been fighting going on, but I'd seen almost none of it. Just more lines on the map table, and later the bloody survivors brought back to the field hospital. Tri-V war, none of it real. The observation satellite had made a pass over the Allan Valley just before dark, and the new pictures were relayed from Garrison. They weren't very clear. There'd been low clouds, enough to cut down the resolution and leave big gaps in my data about the Association forces.

"Number One chopper's coming in, sir," Sergeant Jaski reported. He was a headquarters platoon communications expert, an elderly wizened chap who ran the electronics section with smiles and affection until something went wrong. Then he could be as rough as any NCO in the Fleet.

Number One was Falkenberg's. I wasn't surprised when the captain came in a few minutes later. He'd said he might join the main body if things were quiet up at the pass. I got up from the map table to give him the command seat. It hadn't fit me too well, anyway; I was glad to have someone else take charge.

"Just going over the satellite pix," I told him.

"One reason I came by. Things are going well. When that happens I wonder what I've overlooked." He keyed the map table to give him the current positions of our troops. "Ardwain having any problem with the envelopment?" he asked.

"No, sir."

He grunted and played with the console keys. Then he stared at the satellite pictures. "Mr. Slater, why haven't the Association troops taken the riverbank areas behind the Governor?"

"I don't know, sir."

"Any why didn't His Excellency withdraw by water? He could certainly have gotten out, himself and a few men."

"Didn't want to abandon the militia, sir?"

"Possibly."

I looked at the time. Two hours after dark. The troops were well dug in along the perimeter, except for Ardwain's mobile force moving toward the southern edge of the town.

Falkenberg went through the day's reports and looked up, frowning. "Mr. Slater, why do I have the impression that there's something phony about this whole situation?"

"In what way, sir?"

"It's been too easy. We've been told the Association is a tough outfit, but so far the only opposition has been some infantry screens that withdrew before you made real contact, and the first actual hard fighting was when you reached the town."

"There were the artillery duels, sir."

"Yes. All won by a few exchanges of fire. Doesn't that seem strange?"

"No, sir." I had good reason to know that Deane's lads could do some great shooting. After the support they gave me at the roadblock below Beersheba, I was ready to believe they could do anything. "I hadn't thought about it, sir, but now that you ask—well, it was easy. A couple of exchanges and their guns are quiet."

Falkenberg was nodding. "Knocked out, or merely taken out of action? Looking at this map, I'd say you aren't ready for the second alternative."

"I—"

"You've done well, Lieutenant. It's my nasty suspicious mind. I don't like surprises. Furthermore, why hasn't the Governor asked to be evacuated by water? Why is he sitting there in Allansport?"

"Sir—"

He wouldn't let me finish. "I presume you've reported your positions and plans to the Governor?"

"Certainly, sir."

"And we took the pass with very little effort. Next to no casualties. Yet the Association is certainly aware that we hold it. Why haven't their town forces done something? Run, storm the bluffs and take the Governor for a hostage—*something!*" He straightened in decision. "Sergeant Major!"

"Sir!"

"I want a message taken to Centurion Ardwain. I don't want any possibility of it being intercepted."

"Sir."

"He's to hold up on the envelopment. Send a couple of patrols forward to dig in where they can observe, but keep our forces out of Allansport. He can move around out there and make a lot of noise. I want them to think we've continued the envelopment, but, in fact, Ardwain is to take his troops northwest and dig in no closer than two klicks to the town. They're to do that as quietly and invisibly as possible."

"Yes, sir." Ogilvie went out.

"Insurance, Mr. Slater," Falkenberg said. "Insurance. We didn't need your envelopment."

"Yes, sir."

"Confused, Mister?"

"Yes, sir."

"Just preserving options, Lieutenant. I don't like to commit my forces until I'm certain of my objectives."

"But the objective is to trap the Association forces and neutralize them," I said. "The envelopment would have done that. We wouldn't have to trust to the ranchers to keep them from escaping to the south."

"I understood that, Lieutenant. Now, if you'll excuse me, we've both got work to do."

"Yes, sir." I left the caravan to find another place to work. There was plenty to do. I set up shop in one of the farmhouse rooms and went back to shuffling papers. About an hour later Deane Knowles came in.

"I got the change of orders," he said. "What's up?"

"Damfino. Have a seat? Coffee's over there."

"I'll have some, thanks." He poured himself a cup

and sat across from me. The room had a big wooden table, rough-hewn from a single tree. That table would have been worth a fortune on Earth. Except for a few protected redwoods, I doubted there was a tree that size in the United States.

"Don't you think I ought to know what's going on?" Deane asked. His voice was friendly, but there was a touch of sarcasm in it.

"Bug Falkenberg if you really want answers," I said. "He doesn't tell me anything, either. All I know is he's sent A Company out into the boonies, and when I asked him to let me join my company, he said I was needed here."

"Tell me about it," Deane said.

I described what had happened.

Deane blew on the hot coffee, then took a sip. "You're telling me that Falkenberg thinks we've put our heads in a trap."

"Yes. What do you think?"

"Good point about the artillery. I thought things were going too well myself. Let's adopt his theory and see where it leads."

"You do understand there's only one person who could have set this theoretical trap," I said.

"Yes."

"What possible motive could he have?" I demanded.

Deane shrugged. "Even so, let's see where it leads. We assume for the purposes of discussion that Governor Hugo Swale has entered into a conspiracy with a criminal gang to inflict anything from a defeat to a disaster on the 501st—"

"And you see how silly it sounds," I said. "Too silly to discuss."

"Assume it," Deane insisted. "That means that the Protective Association is fully aware of our positions and our plans. What could they do with that information?"

"That's why it's so stupid," I said. "So what if they know where we are? If they come out and fight, they'll still get a licking. They can't possibly expect to grind up professional troops! They may be great against ranchers and women and children, but this is a battalion of Line Marines."

"A provisional battalion."

"Same thing."

"Is it? Be realistic, Hal. We've had one campaign, a short one. Otherwise, we're still what came here—a random assortment of troops, half of them recruits, another quarter scraped out of guardhouses, commanded by three newlie lieutenants and the youngest captain in the Fleet. Our colonel's a superannuated military policeman, and we've not a quarter of the equipment a regular line battalion carries."

"We're a match for anything a criminal gang can put in the field—"

"A well-armed criminal gang," Deane said. "Hold onto your regimental pride, Hal. I'm not downgrading the 501st. The point is that we may know we're a damned good outfit, but there's not much reason for anyone else to believe it."

"They'll soon have reason to think differently."

"Maybe." Deane continued to study the maps. "Maybe."

THIRTEEN

The night was quiet. I went on patrol about midnight, not to inspect the guard—we could depend on the NCO's for all that—but mostly to see what it was like out there. The troops were cheerful, looking forward to the next day's battles. Even the recruits grinned wolfishly. They were facing a disorganized mob, and we had artillery superiority. They'd pitched tents by maniples, and inside each tent they'd set up their tiny field stoves so there was hot coffee and chicken stew—and they'd found wine in some of the farmhouses. Our bivouac had more the atmosphere of a campout than an army just before a battle.

Underneath it all was the edge that men have when they're going to fight, but it was well hidden. You're sure it's the other guy who'll buy the farm. Never you. Deep down you know better, but you never talk about that.

An hour before dawn every house along the southern edge of Allansport exploded in red fire. In almost the next instant a time-on-target salvo fell just outside the walls. The bombardment continued, sharp thunder in the night, with red flashes barely visible through the thick mist rising up off the river. I ran to the command caravan.

Falkenberg was already there, of course. I doubt if he'd ever gone to bed. Sergeant Jaski had gotten communications with one of the forward patrols.

"Corporal Levine, sir. I'm dug in about five hundred meters outside the walls. Looks like it was mines in the houses, Captain. Then they dropped a hell of a load onto where we'd have been if we'd moved up last night."

"What's your situation, Levine?" Falkenberg demanded.

"Dug in deep, sir. They killed a couple of my squad even so. It's thick out here, sir. Big stuff. Not just mortars."

That was obvious from the sound, even as far away as we were. No light artillery makes that kind of booming sound.

"A moment, Captain," Levine said. There was a long silence. "Can't keep my head up long, Captain. They're still pounding the area. I see movement in the town. Looks like assault troops coming out the gate. The fire's lifting now. Yeah, those are assault troops. A lot of 'em."

"Sergeant Major, put the battalion on alert for immediate advance," Falkenberg said. "Jaski, when's the next daylight pass of the spy satellite over this area?"

"Seventy minutes after daylight, sir."

"Thank you. Levine, you still there?"

"Yes, Captain. There's more troops moving out of Allansport. Goddamn, there's a couple of tanks. Medium jobs, Suslov class, I'd say. I didn't know them bastards had tanks! Where'd they get them?"

"Good question. Levine, keep your head down and stay out of sight. I want you to stay alive."

"Won't fight over those orders, Captain."

"They're breaking out toward the south," Falkenberg said. "Jaski, get me Lieutenant Bonneyman."

"Sir."

"While you're at it, see if you can raise Centurion Cernan at the pass."

"Aye, aye, sir." Jaski worked at the radio for a moment. "No answer from Mr. Bonneyman, sir. Here's Cernan."

"Thank you." Falkenberg paused. "Mr. Slater, stay here for a moment. You'll need instructions. Centurion Cernan, report."

"Not much to report, Captain. Some movement up above us."

"Above you. Hostiles coming *down* the pass?"

"Could be, Captain, but I don't know. I have patrols up that way, but they haven't reported yet."

"Dig in, Cernan," Falkenberg said. "I'll try to send you some reinforcements. You've got to hold that pass no matter which direction it's attacked from."

"Aye, aye, sir."

Falkenberg nodded. The map board was crawling with symbols and lights as reports came in to Jaski's people and they were programmed onto the display. "Wish I had some satellite pix," Falkenberg said. "There's only one logical move the Association can be making at this point."

He was talking to himself. Maybe he wasn't. Maybe he thought I understood him, but I didn't.

"In any event, we have the only sizable military force on the entire planet," Falkenberg said. "We can't risk its destruction."

"But we've got to relieve Bonneyman and the ranchers," I protested. I didn't mention Kathryn. Falkenberg might think it was just a personal problem.

Maybe it was. "Those tanks are headed south, right for their lines."

"I know. Jaski, keep trying to get Bonneyman."

"Sir!"

Outside the trumpets were sounding "On Full Kits." Brady's sang louder than the rest.

"And we must rescue the Governor," Falkenberg said. "Indeed, we must." He came to a decision. "Jaski, get me Mr. Wan Loo."

While Jaski used the radio, Falkenberg said, "I want you to talk to him, Mr. Slater. He has met you and he has never met me. His first impulse will be to rush to the aid of his friends in the south. He must not do that. His forces, what there are of them, will be far more useful as reinforcements for Centurion Cernan at the pass."

"Mr. Wan Loo, sir," Jaski said.

Falkenberg handed me the mike.

"I don't have time to explain," I said. "You're to take everything you've got and move up to the pass. There are mixed Marine and militia units holding it, and there's a chance Association forces are moving down the pass toward them. Centurion Cernan is in command up there, and he'll need help."

"But what is happening?" Wan Loo asked.

"The Association forces in Allansport have broken loose and are heading south," I said.

"But our friends to the south—"

Falkenberg took the mike. "This is Captain John Christian Falkenberg. We'll assist your friends, but we can do nothing if the forces coming down the pass are not contained. The best way you can help your friends is to see that no fresh Association troops get into this valley."

There was a long pause. "You would not abandon us, Captain?"

"No. We won't abandon you," Falkenberg said.

"Then I have assurances from two honorable men. We will help your friends, Captain. And go with God."

"Thank you. Out." He gave the mike back to Jaski. "Me, I'd rather have a couple of anti-tank guns—or, better still, tanks of our own. How's Old Beastly?"

"Still running, sir." Old Beastly was the 501st's only tank, a relic of the days when CD regulars had come to Arrarat. It was kept going by constant maintenance.

"Where the devil are the Protective Association people getting fuel for tanks?" Falkenberg said. "To hell with it. Sergeant Major, I want Centurion Ardwain to take two platoons of A Company and Old Beastly. Their mission is to link up with Governor Swale. They're to attack through the north end of the town along the riverbank, and they're to move cautiously."

"Captain, that's my company," I said. "Shouldn't I go with them?"

"No. I have a number of operations to perform, and I'll need help. Don't you trust Ardwain?"

"Of course I trust him, sir—"

"Then let him do his job. Sergeant Major, Ardwain's mission is to simulate at least a company. He's to keep the men spread out and moving around. The longer it takes for the enemy to tumble to how small his force is, the better. And he's not to take chances. If they gang up on him, he can run like hell."

"Sir," Ogilvie said. He turned to a waiting runner.

"Ardwain's got a radio, sir," I said.

"Sure he has." Falkenberg's voice was conversational. "Know much about the theory of the scrambler codes we use, Mr. Slater?"

"Well, no, sir—"

"You know this much: in theory any message can be recorded off the air and unscrambled with a good enough computer."

"Yes, sir. But the only computer on Arrarat that could do that is ours, in Garrison."

"And the Governor's in the palace at Harmony," Falkenberg said. "And those two are the ones we know about."

"Sir, you're saying that Governor—"

"No," he interrupted. "I have said nothing at all. I merely choose to be certain that my orders are not intercepted. Jaski, where the hell is Bonneyman?"

"Still trying to raise him, sir."

"Any word from Miss Malcolm or the other ranchers in the southern area?"

"No, sir."

More information appeared on the map board. Levine was still reporting. There were only the two tanks, but a sizable infantry force had come out of Allansport and was headed south along the river-bank. If Levine was right, there'd been more troops in Allansport than we'd ever suspected.

"I have Lieutenant Bonneyman, sir."

"Thank God." Falkenberg grabbed the mike. "Mr. Bonneyman, nearly one thousand hostiles have broken free from Allansport and are moving south. They have with them at least two medium tanks and an appreciable artillery train. Are you well dug in?"

"Yes, sir. We'll hold them."

"The devil, you will. Not with riflemen against that."

"We have to hold, sir," Louis said. "Miss Malcolm and an escort moved about twenty kilometers south during the night in the hopes of raising more reinforcements. She was not successful, but she has reports of hostile activities south of us. At least two, possibly more, groups of Association forces are moving north. We must hold them or they'll break through and link up with the Allansport groups."

"One moment," Falkenberg said. "Sergeant Major, I want helicopter observation of the area to the south of Lieutenant Bonneyman and his ranchers. Send Stragoff. He's to stay at high altitude, but it's vital that I find out what's coming north at us out of Denisburg. All right, Mr. Bonneyman. At the moment you don't know what you're facing."

"No, sir, but I'm in a pretty good position. Rifle pits, and we're strengthening the southern perimeter."

"All right. You're probably safer there than anywhere else. If you get into trouble, your escape route is east, toward the river. I'm bringing the 501st around the town. We'll skirt it wide to stay away from their artillery. Then we'll cut in toward the river and stay right along the bank until we reach your position. If necessary, our engineers can throw up a pontoon bridge and we'll go out across the river to escape."

"Do we need to run, Captain?" Louis sounded dismayed.

"As I have explained to Mr. Slater, our prime objective is to retain the 501st as a fighting unit. Be prepared to withdraw eastward on command, Mr. Bonneyman. Until then, you're to hold that position no matter what happens, and it's likely to be rough."

"Can do, Captain."

"Excellent. Now, what about Miss Malcolm?"

"I don't know where she is, sir. I can send a patrol—"

"No. You have no forces to spare. If you can get a message to her, have her rejoin you if that's possible. Otherwise, she's on her own. You understand your orders, Mister?"

"Yes, sir."

"Excellent. Out."

"So Kathryn's expendable," I said.

"Anyone is expendable, Mister. Sergeant Major, have Stragoff listen on Miss Malcolm's frequency. If he can locate her, he can try to evacuate her from the southern area, but he is not to compromise the reconnaissance mission in doing it."

"Sir."

"You are one hard-nosed son-of-a-bitch," I said.

His voice was calm as he said, "Mister, I get paid to take responsibilities, and at the moment I'm earning my keep. I'll overlook that remark. Once."

And if I say anything else, I'll be in arrest while my troops are fighting. Got you. "What are my orders, sir?"

"For the moment you're to lead the forward elements of the 501st. I want the battalion to move in column around the town, staying outside artillery range. When you've reached a point directly southwest of Allansport, halt the lead elements and gather up the battalion as I send it to you. I'll stay here until this has been accomplished. I still must report to the Governor and I want the daylight satellite pictures."

I looked at my watch. Incredibly, it was still a quarter-hour before dawn. A lot had happened in the last forty-five minutes. When I left the caravan, Falkenberg was playing games on the map board. More bloodless battles, with glowing lights and wriggling lines crawling across the map at lightning speed, simulations of hours of bloody combat and death and agony.

And what the hell are you accomplishing? I thought. The computer can't give better results than the input data, and your intelligence about the hostiles is plain lousy. How many Association toops are coming down the pass toward Centurion Cernan? No data. How many more are in those converging columns moving toward Louis and Kathryn and their ranchers? Make a guess. What are their objectives? Another guess. Guess and guess again, and Kathryn's out there, and instead of rescuing her, we're keeping the battalion intact. I wanted to mutiny, to go to Kathryn with all the men I could get to follow me, but I wasn't going to do that. I blinked back tears. We had a mission, and Falkenberg was probably right. He was going to the aid of the ranchers, and that's what Kathryn would want. She'd pledged her honor to those people, and it was up to us to make that good. Maybe Stragoff will find her, I thought. Maybe.

I went to my room and let Hartz hang equipment onto my uniform. It was time to move out, and I was glad of something, anything, to do.

FOURTEEN

The valley was filled with a thick white mist. The fog boiled out of the river and flowed across the valley floor. In the two hours since dawn, the 501st had covered nine kilometers. The battalion was strung out in a long column of men and mules and wagons on muddy tracks that had once been roads and now had turned into sloppy gunk. The men strained at ropes to pull the guns and ammunition wagons along, and when we found oxen or mules in the fields, we hitched them up as well. The rainstorm that had soaked us two days before at Beersheba had passed across the Allan Valley, and the fields were squishy marshlands.

Out in the distance we could hear the sound of guns: Ardwain's column, the Allansport garrison trying to get through Louis's position—or someone else a world away. In the fog we couldn't know. The sound had no direction, and out here there was no battle, only mud.

There were no enemies here in the valley. There weren't any friends, either. There were only refugees, pathetic families with possessions piled on their mules and oxen, or carried in their arms. They didn't know where they were going, and I had no place to send them. Sometimes we passed farms, and we could see women and children staring at us from the partly open doors or from behind shuttered windows. Their eyes had no expression in them. The sound of the guns over the horizon, and the curses of the men as they fought to move our equipment through the mud; more curses as men whipped oxen we'd found and hitched to the wagons; shrill cries from farmers protesting the loss of their stock; everything dripping wet in white swirling fog, all blended together into a long nightmare of outraged feelings and senselessness. I felt completely alone, alien to all this. Where were the people we'd come to set free?

We reached the map point Falkenberg had designated, and the troops rested in place while the rest of the column caught up with us. The guns were just moving in when Falkenberg's command caravan roared up. The ground-effects machine could move across the muddy fields with no problems, while we had to sweat through them.

He sent for Deane Knowles and had us both come into the caravan. Then he sent out all the NCO's and enlisted men. The three of us were alone with the map table.

"I've held off explaining what I've been doing until the last minute," he said. "As it is, this is for your ears only. If something happens, I want someone to know I haven't lost my mind."

"Yes, sir," I said. Deane and I looked at each other.

"Some background," Falkenberg said. "There's been something peculiar about the Allan Valley situation for years. The convict groups have been too well armed, for a beginning. Governor Swale was too eager to recognize them as a legitimate local government. I think both of you have remarked on that before."

Deane and I looked at each other again.

"This morning's satellite pictures," Falkenberg said. "There's too much mist to show any great details, but there are some clear patches. This strip was taken in the area south of Mr. Bonneyman. I invite your comments."

He handed us the photos. Most were of patches of mist, with the ground below completely invisible. Others showed patches where the mist was thin, or there wasn't any. "Nothing at all," Deane said.

"Precisely," Falkenberg said. "Yet we have reports of troop movements in that area. It is as if the hostiles knew when the satellite would be overhead, and avoided clear patches."

"As well they might," Deane said. "It shouldn't be hard to work out the ephemeris of the spy-eye."

"Correct. Now look at the high resolution enlargements of those clear areas."

We looked again. "The roads are chewed up," I said. "Mud and ruts. A lot of people and wagons have passed over them."

"And recently, I'd say." Falkenberg nodded in satisfaction. If this had been a test, we'd passed. "Now another datum. I have had Sergeant Jaski's people monitoring all transmissions from Allansport. It may or may not be significant that shortly after every communication between 501st headquarters and outlying commands, there has been a transmission from the Governor to the palace at Harmony— and, within half an hour, a reply. Not an immediate reply, gentlemen, but a reply within half an hour. And shortly after that, there is traffic on the frequencies the Association forces use."

There wasn't anything to say to that. The only explanation made no sense.

"Now, let's see what the hostiles have in mind," Falkenberg said. "They besiege the Governor in Allansport. Our initial orders are to send a force to relieve him. We don't know what they would have done, but instead we devised a complex plan to trap them. We take the initial steps, and what happens? The hostiles invite us to continue. They do nothing. Later we learn that a considerable force, possibly the major part of their strength, is marching northward. Their evident objective is Mr. Bonneyman's mixed group of Marines and ranchers. I point out that the elimination of those ranchers would be significant to the Association. They would not only be rid of potential opposition to their rule, but I think it would in future be impossible to persuade any significant group of ranchers to rise against them. The Association would be the only possible government in the Allan Valley."

"Yes, sir, but why?" Deane said. "What could be . . . why would Governor Swale cooperate with them?"

"We'll leave that for the moment, Mr. Knowles. One thing at a time. Now for the present situation. Centurion Ardwain has done an excellent job of simulating a large force cautiously advancing into Allansport from the north. Governor Swale seems convinced that we've committed at least half our strength there. I have further informed him that we will now bring the balance of the 501st from its present position directly east to the riverbank, where we will once again divide our troops, half going south to aid Mr. Bonneyman, the other half moving into the town. The Governor thought that a splendid plan. Have you an opinion, Mr. Slater?"

"It's the dumbest thing I ever heard of," I said. "Especially if he thinks you've already divided the force! If you do that, you'll be inviting defeat in detail."

"Precisely," Falkenberg said. "Of course Governor Swale has no military background."

"He doesn't need one to know that plan's a bust," I said. "Lousy traitor—"

"No accusations," Falkenberg said. "We've no proof of anything. In any event, I am making the assumption that the Association is getting decoded copies of all my transmissions. I don't need to know how they get them. You'll remember that whenever you use radio signals that might be overheard."

"Yes, sir." Deane looked thoughtful. "That limits our communications somewhat."

"Yes. I hope that won't matter. Next problem. Under my assumption, the hostiles expect me to send a force eastward toward the river. That expectation must be met. I need Mr. Knowles to handle the artillery. It leaves you, Mr. Slater. I want you to take a platoon and simulate two companies with it. You'll send back a stream of reports, as if you're the main body of the battalion reporting to me at a headquarters left safely out of the combat zone." Falkenberg grinned slightly. "To the best of my knowledge, Irina's opinion of me is shared by her father. He won't find it at all hard to believe that I'm avoiding a combat area."

"But what if I really have a message?" I asked.

"You're familiar with O'Grady drill?" Falkenberg asked.

"Yes, sir." O'Grady drill is a form of torture devised by drill sergeants. You're supposed to obey only the commands that begin with "O'Grady says:." Then the sergeant snaps out a string of orders.

"We'll play that little game," Falkenberg said. "Now your mission is to get to the river, make a short demonstration, as if you're about to attack the southern edge of Allansport, and then move directly south, away from the town, until you link up with Mr. Bonneyman. You will then aid in his defense until you are relieved."

"But—Captain, you're assuming they know your orders."

He nodded. "Of course they'll put out an ambush. In this fog it will be a natural thing for them to do. Since they'll assume you have a much larger force with you, they'll probably use all the force that left Allansport this morning. I can't think they're stupid enough to try it with less."

"And we're to walk into it," I said.

"Yes. With your eyes open, but walk into it. You're bait, Mr. Slater. Get out there and wiggle."

I remembered an old comic strip. I quoted a line from it. "Don't much matter whether you catch a fish or not; once you been used for bait, you ain't much good for nothing else nohow."

"Maybe," Falkenberg said. "Maybe. But I remind you that you'll be keeping a major column of Association forces off Mr. Bonneyman's back."

"We will so long as we survive—"

"Yes. So I'll expect you to survive as long as possible."

"Can't quarrel with those orders, Captain."

The fog was thicker when we reached the river. The troops were strung out along almost a full kilometer route, each maniple isolated from the others in the dripping-white blanket that lay across the valley. The troops were enjoying themselves, with monitors reporting as if they were platoon sergeants, and corporals playing centurion. They kept up a steady stream of chatter on the radio, while two men back at Falkenberg's headquarters sent orders that we paid no attention to. So far it was easy enough, because we hadn't run into anything at all.

"There's the city wall." Roszak pointed leftward. I could barely see a darker shape in the fog. "We'll take a quick look over. All right, Lieutenant?"

"Yes. Be careful."

"Always am, sir. Brady, bring your squad. Let's see what's over there." They vanished into the fog.

It seemed like hours, but it was only a few minutes before Brady returned. "Nothing, sir. Nothing and nobody, at least not close to the walls. May be a lot of them farther in. I got a feeling."

Roszak's voice came into my command set. "Moved fifty meters in. No change from what Brady reported."

"Did he have your feeling, Brady?" I asked.

"Yes, sir."

I switched the set back on. "Thank you, Roszak. Rejoin your company."

"Aye, aye, sir."

There were distant sounds of firing from the north. Ardwain's group was doing a good job of simulating a company. They were still moving into the town house by house. I wondered if he was running into opposition, or if that was all his own doing. He was supposed to go cautiously, and his men might be shooting up everything in sight. They were making a lot of noise. "Get me Falkenberg," I told Hartz.

"Yes, Mr. Slater?"

"Captain, Monitor O'Grady reports the south end of the town has been abandoned. I can hear the A Company combat team up at the north end, but I don't know what opposition they've encountered."

"Very light, Mister. You leave a company to assist A Company just in case, and continue south. Exactly as planned, Mr. Slater. No change. Got that?"

"Yes, sir."

"Having any trouble with the guns?"

"A little, sir. Roads are muddy. It's tough going, but we're moving."

"Excellent. Carry on, then. Out."

And that, I told myself, is that. I told off a monitor to dig in just outside the town and continue making reports. "You've just become B Company centurion," I said.

He grinned. "Yes, sir. Save a few of 'em for me."

"I'll do that, Yokura. Good luck." I waved the rest of my command down the road. We were strung out in a long column. The fog was a little thinner. Now I could see over twenty meters before the world was blotted out in swirling white mist.

What's the safest way to walk into an ambush? I asked myself. The safest way is not to do it. Bar that solution and you don't have a lot of choices. I used the helmet projector to show me a map of the route.

The first test was a hill just outside of town: Hill 509, called the Rockpile, a warren of jumbled boulders and flinty ledges. It dominated the road into the southern gate of Allansport. Whoever owned it controlled traffic into and out of the town.

If the Association only wanted to block us from moving south, that's where they'd have their strong point. If they were out to ambush the whole battalion, they'd leave it bare and set the trap farther on. Either way, they'd never expect me to go past it without having a look.

Four kilometers past the Rockpile there was a string of low hills. The road ran through a valley below them. It was an ideal place for an ambush. That's where they'll be, I decided. Only they must know we'll expect them to be along there somewhere. Bait should wiggle, but it shouldn't too obviously be bait. How would I act if I really had most of a battalion with me?

Send a strong advance guard, of course. An ad-

vance guard about as strong as the whole force I've
got. Anything less won't make any sense.

"Roszak, start closing them up. Leave the wagons
and half a dozen men with radios strung out along
the line of march, and get everyone else up here.
We'll form up as an advance guard and move south."

"Aye, aye, sir."

When I had the troops assembled, I led them up
on the Rockpile. Nothing there, of course. I'd gauged
it right. They were waiting for us up ahead.

Roszak nudged me and turned his head slightly to
the right. I nodded, carefully. "Don't point, Sergeant. I saw something move up there myself."

We had reached the hills.

"Christ, what are they waiting for?" Roszak muttered.

"For the rest of the battalion. They don't want us;
they want the whole 501st."

"Yes, sir."

We moved on ahead. The fog was lifting; visibility
was over fifty meters already. It wouldn't be long
before it would be obvious there weren't any troops
following me, despite the loud curses and the squeals
of wagon wheels back there. It's amazing how much
noise a couple of wagons can make if the troops work
at it.

To hell with it, I thought. We've got to find a good
position and try to hold it. It'll do no good to keep
walking farther into their trap. There was a rocky
area ahead. It wasn't perfect, but it was the best spot
I'd seen in half an hour. I nudged Roszak. "When we
get up to there, start waving the men off into the
rocks. The fog's thicker there."

"What if there's hostiles there already?" Roszak
demanded.

"Then we'll fight for the ground, but I doubt they'll

be there. I expect they've been moving out of our way as we advance. They still think there's a column a whole klick long behind us." Sound confident, I told myself. "We'll take up a defensive perimeter in there and wait the war out."

"Sure." Roszak moved to his right and spoke to the next man. The orders were passed along the line.

Three more minutes, I told myself. Three minutes and we'll at least have some cover. The area I'd chosen was a saddle, a low pass between the hills to either side of us. Not good, but better than the road. I could feel rifles aimed at me from the rocks above, but I saw nothing but grotesque shapes, boulders dripping in the fog. We climbed higher, moving steadily toward the place I'd chosen.

Maybe there's nobody up there watching at all. They may be on the other side of the valley. You only saw one man. Maybe not even a man. Just something moving. A wild animal. A dog. A blowing patch of fog.

Whatever it was, I can't take this much longer. You don't have to. Another minute. That boulder up there, the big one. When you reach it, you've finished. Don't run. Keep it slow—

"All right, you can fall out and take a break!" I shouted. "Hartz, tell the column to rest in place. We'll take ten. Companies should close up and gather in the stragglers. They'll assemble here after the break."

"Zur."

"Better get a perimeter guard out, Sergeant."

"Sir," Roszak called.

"Corporal Brady, how about a little coffee? You can set up the stove in the lee of that rock."

"Right, Lieutenant."

The men vanished into the fog. There were scrambling noises as they found hiding places. I moved out of the open and hunkered down in the rocks with Corporal Brady. "You didn't really have to make coffee," I said.

"Why not, Lieutenant? We have a while to wait, don't we?"

"I hope so, Corporal. I hope so. But that fog's lifting fast."

Ten minutes later we heard the guns. It was difficult to tell the direction of the sound in the thick fog, but I thought they were ahead of us, far to the south. There was no way to estimate the range.

"O'Grady message from Captain Falkenberg," Hartz said. "Lieutenant Bonneyman's group is under heavy attack from the south."

"Acknowledge." From the south. That meant the columns coming north out of Denisburg had made contact with Louis's ranchers. Falkenberg had guessed that much right. Maybe this whole screwy plan would work, after all. "Anything new on Ardwain's situation?"

"No messages, zur."

I thumbed my command set to the general frequency. "All units of the 501st, there is heavy fighting to the south. Assemble immediately. We'll be moving south to provide fire support. Get those guns rolling right now."

There was a chorus of radio answers. Only a dozen men, but they sounded like hundreds. I'd have been convinced it was a battalion combat team. I was congratulating myself when a shaft of sunlight broke through the mist and fell on the ground at my feet.

FIFTEEN

Once the sun had broken through, the fog lifted fast. In seconds visibility went from fifty meters to a hundred, then two hundred. In minutes the road for a kilometer north of us was visible—and empty. One wagon struggled along it, and far back in the distance a single man carried a radio.

"O'Grady says hit the dirt!" I yelled. "Hartz, tell Falkenberg the deception's over."

And still there was nothing. I took out my glasses and examined the rocks above and behind us. They were boiling with activity. "Christ," I said. "Roszak, we've run into the whole Allansport outfit. Damned near a thousand men! Dig in and get your heads down!"

A mortar shell exploded on the road below. Then another, and then a salvo. Not bad shooting, I said to myself. Of course it didn't hit anything, because there was nothing to hit except the one wagon, but they had it registered properly. If we'd been down there, we'd have had it.

Rifle bullets zinged overhead. The Association troops

were firing at last. I tried to imagine the feelings of the enemy commander, and I found myself laughing. He'd waited patiently all this time for us to walk into his trap, and all he'd caught was something less than a platoon. He was going to be mad.

He was also going to chew up my sixty men, two mortars, and four light machine guns. It would take him a little time, though. I'd picked a good spot to wait for him. Now that the fog had cleared, I saw it was a better place than I'd guessed from the map. We had reasonably clear fields of fire, and the rocks were large and sturdy. They'd have to come in and get us. All we had to do was keep our heads down.

No point in deception anymore. "O'Grady says stay loose and let 'em come to us."

There was a chorus of shouted responses. Then Brady's trumpet sounded, beginning with "On Full Kits" and running through half the calls in the book before he settled onto the Line Marines' March. A favorite, I thought. Damned right. Then I heard the whistle of incoming artillery, and I dove for the tiny shelter between my rocks as barrage after barrage of heavy artillery dropped onto our position.

Riflemen swarmed down onto the road behind me. My radiomen and the two wagoneers were cut down in seconds. At least a company of Association troops started up the gentle slope toward us.

The Association commander made his first mistake then. His artillery had been effective enough for making us keep our heads down, but the rocks gave us good cover and we weren't taking many casualties. When the Association charged us, their troops held back until the artillery fire lifted. It takes experienced non-coms and a lot of discipline to get troops to take casualties from their own artillery. It pays off, but our attackers didn't know or believe it.

They were too far away when the artillery fire

lifted. My lads were out of their hiding places in an instant. They poured fire on the advancing troops—rifles and the light machine guns, then both mortars. Few of the enemy had combat armor, and our fire was devastating.

"Good men," Hartz grunted. "They keep coming."

They were, but not for long. Too many of them were cut down. They swept to within fifty meters, wavered, and dropped back, some dragging their wounded with them, others running for it. When the attack was broken, we dropped back into the rocks to wait for the next barrage. "Score one for the Line Marines," I called.

Brady answered with the final fanfare from the March. "And there's none that can face us—"

"They won't try that again," Roszak said. He grinned with satisfaction. "Lads are doing right well, Mr. Slater."

"Well, indeed."

Our area was quiet, but there were sounds of heavy fighting in the south: artillery, rifle and machine-gun fire, mortars and grenades. It sounded louder, as if it were coming closer to us. Louis and his commando of ranchers were facing big odds. I wondered if Kathryn were with him.

"They'll try infiltration next," Roszak predicted.

"What makes you think so?" Hartz asked.

"No discipline. After what happened last time, they'll never get a full attack going."

"No, they will have one more try in force. Perhaps two," Hartz argued.

"Never. Bet on it? Tomorrow's wine ration."

"Done," Hartz said. He was quiet for a moment, then handed me the handset. "Captain Falkenberg."

"Thank you. Yes, Captain?"

"O'Grady says the O'Grady drill is over. Understood?"

"Yes, sir."

"What's your situation?"

"We're in the saddle notch of Hill 239, seven klicks south of Allansport," I said. "Holding all right for now, but we're surrounded. Most of the hostiles are between us and Allansport. They let us right through for the ambush. They've tried one all-out attack and that didn't work. Roszak and Hartz are arguing over what they'll try next."

"How long can you hold?"

"Depends on what losses they're willing to take to get us out of here."

"You don't have to hold long," Falkenberg said. "A lot has happened. Ardwain broke through to the Governor and brought him out, but he ran into a strong force in Allansport. There's more coming over the bridge from the east side of the river."

"Sounds like they're bringing up everything they have."

"They are, and we're beating all of it. The column that moved north from Denisburg ran into Bonney-man's group. They deployed to break through that, and we circled around to their west and hit them in the flank. They didn't expect us. Your maneuver fooled them completely. They thought the 501st was with you until it was too late. They know better now, but we've broken them. Of course, there's a lot more of them than of us, and we couldn't hold them. They've broken through between Bonneyman and the river, and you're right in their path."

"How truly good."

"I think you'd do well to get out of their way," Falkenberg said. "I doubt you can stop them."

"If they link up with the Allansport force, they'll get away across the bridge. I can't hold them, but if you can get some artillery support here, I can spot for the guns. We might delay them."

"I was going to suggest that," Falkenberg said. "I've sent Ardwain and the Governor's escort toward that hill outside Allansport—the Rockpile. It looks like a dominant position."

"It is, sir. I've seen it. If we held that, we could keep this lot from getting into Allansport. We might bag the whole lot."

"Worth a try, anyway," Falkenberg said. "Provided you can hold on. It will be nearly an hour before I can get artillery support to you."

"We'll hold, sir."

"Good luck."

Roszak lost his wine ration. They tried one more assault. Two squads of Association troops got within twenty meters of our position before we threw them back. Of my sixty men, I had fewer than thirty effectives when it was over.

That was their last try, though. Shortly after, they regrouped. The elements which had been south of us had already skirted around the hills to join the main body, and now the whole group was moving north. They were headed for Allansport.

The sounds of fighting to the south were coming closer all the time. Falkenberg had Deane moving parallel to the Association troops, racing to get close enough to give us support, but it wouldn't arrive in time.

I sent our wounded up the hill away from the road with orders to dig in and lie low. The rest of us followed the retreating force. We were now sandwiched between the group ahead of us and the Denisburg column behind.

The first elements of Association forces were headed up the Rockpile when Deane came in range. He was still six kilometers southeast of us, long range and long time of flight, but we were in a good position to spot for him. I called in the first salvo on the advancing Association troops. The shells went beyond their target, and before I could walk them back down the hill, the Association forces retreated.

"They'll send another group around behind the hill," Roszak said. "We'll never stop them."

"No." So damned near. A few minutes' difference and we'd have bagged them all. The column Falkenberg was chasing was now no more than two kilometers south of us and moving fast.

"Hold one," Deane said. "I've got a Corporal Dangier calling in. Claims to be in position to spot targets for me."

"He's one of the wounded we left behind," I said. "He can see the road from his position, all right, but he won't last long once they know we've got a spotter in position to observe them."

"Do I fire the mission?" Deane demanded.

"Yes." Scratch Corporal Dangier, who had a girl in Harmony and a wife on Earth.

"I'll leave one gun at your disposal," Deane said. "I'm putting the rest on Dangier's mission."

A few minutes later we heard the artillery falling on the road behind us. That would play hell with the Association retreat. It kept up for ten minutes; then Deane called in again. "Can't raise Dangier any longer."

"No. There's nothing we can do here. They're staying out of sight. I'll call in some fire in places that might do some good, but it's shooting blind."

I amused myself with that for a while. It was frustrating. Once that force got to the top of the Rockpile, the route into Allansport would be secure. I was still cursing when Hartz shouted urgently.

"Centurion Ardwain on the line, sir."

"Ardwain, where are you?"

"Less than a klick west of you, Lieutenant. We

moved around the edge of the town. Can't get inside without support. Militia won't try it, anyway."

"How many Marines do you have?" I demanded.

"About eighty effective. And Old Beastly."

"By God! Ardwain, move in fast. We'll join you as you come by. We're going right up to the top of the Rockpile and sit there until Falkenberg gets here. With Deane's artillery support we can hold that hill."

"Aye, aye, sir. We're coming."

"Let's go!" I shouted. "Who's been hit and can't run?"

No one answered. "Sergeant Roszak took one in the leg an hour ago, Lieutenant," Hartz said.

"I can still travel," Roszak said.

"Bullshit. You'll stay here and spot artillery for us. All the walking wounded stay with him. The rest of you get moving. We want to be in position when Centurion Ardwain comes."

"But—"

"Shut up and soldier, Roszak." I waved and we moved down from our low hilltop. We were panting when we got to the base of the Rockpile. There were already Association forces up there. I didn't know how many. We had to get up there before more joined them. The way up just ahead of me was clear, because it was in direct view of Roszak and his artillery spotters. We could use it and they couldn't.

I waved the men forward. Even a dozen of us on top of the Rockpile might be enough if Ardwain came up fast. We started up. Two men went down, then another, and my troops began to look around for shelter. I couldn't blame them, but I couldn't let them do it. Getting up that hill had become the only thing in my life. I had to get them moving again.

"Brady!" I shouted. "Corporal, sound the charge!"

The trumpet notes sang out. A monitor whipped out a banner and waved it above his head. I shouted

"Follow me!" and ran up the hill. Then a mortar shell exploded two meters away. I had time to see bright red blotches spurt across my trousers legs and to wonder if that was my own blood; then I fell. The battle noises dimmed out.

"Lieutenant! Mr. Slater!"

I was in the bottom of a well. It was dark down there, and it hurt to look up at the light. I wanted to sink back into the well, but someone at the top was shouting at me. "Mr. Slater!"

"He's coming around, Centurion."

"He's got to, Crisp! Mr. Slater!"

There were people all around me. I couldn't see them very clearly, but I could recognize the voice. "Yes, Centurion."

"Mr. Slater," Ardwain said. "The Governor says we shouldn't take the hill! What do we do, sir?"

It didn't make sense. Where am I? I wondered. I had just sense enough not to ask. Everybody asks that, I thought. Why does everybody ask that? But I don't know—

I was pulled to a sitting position. My eyes managed to focus again, just for a moment. I was surrounded by people and rocks. Big rocks. Then I knew where I was. I'd passed these rocks before. They were at the base of the hill. Rocks below the Rockpile.

"What's that? Don't take the hill?" I said.

"Yes, sir—"

"Lieutenant, I have ordered your men to pull back. There are not enough to take this hill, and there's no point in wasting them."

That wasn't the Governor, but I'd heard the voice before. Trevor. Colonel Trevor of the militia. He'd been with Swale at the staff meeting back at Beersheba. Bits of the staff meeting came back to me, and

I tried to remember more of them. Then I realized that was silly. The staff meeting wasn't important, but I couldn't think. What was important? There was something I had to do.

Get up the hill. I had to get up the hill. "Get me on my feet, Centurion."

"Sir—"

"Do it!" I was screaming. "I'm going up there. We have to take the Rockpile."

"You heard the company commander!" Ardwain shouted. "Move out!"

"Slater, you don't know what you're saying!" Trevor shouted.

I ignored him. "I've got to see," I said. I tried to get up, but my legs weren't working. Nothing happened when I tried to move them. "Lift me where I can see," I said.

"Sir—"

"Crisp, don't argue with me. Do it."

"You're crazy, Slater!" Trevor shouted. "Delirious. Sergeant Crisp, put him down. You'll kill him."

The medics hauled me to the edge of the boulder patch. Ardwain was leading men up the hill. Not just Marines, I saw. The militia had followed, as well. Insane, something whispered in the back of my mind. All insane. It's a disease, and they've caught it, too. I pushed the thought away.

They were falling, but they were still moving forward as they fell. I didn't know if they'd get to the top.

"You wanted to see!" Trevor shouted. "Now you've seen it! You can't send them up there. It's suicide, and they won't even listen to me! You've got to call them back, Slater. Make them retreat."

I looked at the fallen men. Some were just ahead of me. They hadn't even gotten twenty meters. There was one body blown in half. Something bright lay near it. I saw what it was and turned to Trevor.

"Retreat, Colonel? See that? Our trumpeter was killed sounding the charge. I don't know how to order a retreat."

SIXTEEN

I was deep in the well again, and it was dark, and I was afraid. They reached down into it after me, trying to pull me up, and I wanted to come. I knew I'd been in there a long time, and I wanted out, because I could hear Kathryn calling for me. I reached for her hand, but I couldn't find it. I remember shouting, but I don't know what I said. The nightmare went on for a long time.

Then it was daytime. The light was orange-red, very bright, and the walls were splashed with the orange light. I tried to move my head.

"Doc!" someone shouted. His voice was very loud. "Hal?"

"I can't see you," I said. "Where are you, Kathryn? Where are you?"

"I'm here, Hal. I'll always be here."

And then it was dark again, but it wasn't so lonely in there.

I woke up several times after that. I couldn't talk much, and when I did I don't suppose I made much sense, but finally things were clear. I was in the hospital in Garrison, and I'd been there for weeks. I wasn't sure just how long. Nobody would tell me anything, and they talked in hushed tones so that I was sure I was dying, but I didn't.

"What the hell's wrong with me?" I demanded.

"Just take it easy, young fellow." He had a white coat, thick glasses, and a brown beard with white hairs in it.

"Who the hell are you?"

"That's Dr. Cechi," Kathryn told me.

"Well, why won't he tell me what's wrong with me?"

"He doesn't want to worry you."

"Worry me? Do you think not knowing gives peace of mind? Tell me."

"All right," Cechi said. "Nothing permanent. Understand that first. Nothing permanent, although it's going to take a while to fix you up. We almost lost you a couple of times, you know. Multiple perforations of the gut, two broken vertebrae, compound fracture of the left femur, and assorted scrapes, punctures, bruises, abrasions, and contusions. Not to mention almost complete exsanguination when they brought you in. It's nothing we can't fix, but you're going to be here a while, Captain." He was holding my arm, and I felt pressure there, a hypo-spray. "You just go to sleep and we'll tell you the rest tomorrow."

"But—" Whatever I was going to say never got out. I sank back, but it wasn't into the well. It was just sleep, and I could tell the difference.

The next time I awoke, Falkenberg was there. He grinned at me.

I grinned back. "Hi, Captain."

"Major. You're the captain."

"Uh? Run that past—"

"Just brevet promotions, but Harrington thinks they'll stick."

"We must have won."

"Oh, yeah." He sat where I could see him. His eyes looked pale blue in that light. "Lieutenant Ardwain took the Rockpile, but he said it was all your doing."

"Lieutenant Ardwain. Lot of promotions out of this," I said.

"Some. The Association no longer exists as an organized military force. Your girl's friends are in control. Wan Loo is the acting president, or supervisor, or whatever they call him. Governor Swale's not too happy about it, but officially he has to be. He didn't like endorsing Harrington's report, either, but he had no choice."

"But he's a lousy traitor. Why's he still Governor?"

"Act your age, Captain." There wasn't any humor in Falkenberg's voice now. "We have no proof. I know the story, if you'd like to hear it. In fact, you'd better. You're popular enough with the Fleet, but there'll be elements of the Grand Senate that'll hate your guts."

"Tell me."

"Swale has always been part of the Bronson faction," Falkenberg said. "The Bronson family is big in Dover Mineral Development Inc. Seems there's more to this place than either American Express or Kennicott ever knew. Dover found out and tried to buy mineral rights. The holy Joes wouldn't sell—especially the farmers like Wan Loo and Seeton. They don't want industrial development here, and it was obvious to Swale that they wouldn't sell any mining rights to Dover. Swale's policy has been to help groups like the Association in return for their signatures on mining rights contracts. If enough of those outfits are recognized as legitimate local governments, there won't be any trouble over the contracts. You can probably figure out the rest."

"Maybe it's my head," I told him, "but I can't. What the devil did he let us into the valley for, then? Why did he go down there at all?"

"Just because they signed over some mining rights didn't make them his slaves. They were trying to jack up the grain prices. If the Harmony merchants complained loud enough, Swale wouldn't be governor here, and what use would he be to Dover then? He had to put some pressure on them—enough to make them sell, not so much that they'd be thrown out"

"Only we threw them out," I said.

"Only we threw them out. This time. Don't imagine that it's over."

"It has to be over," I said. "He couldn't pull that again."

"Probably he won't. Bronson hasn't much use for failures. I expect Governor Swale will shortly be on his way to a post as First Secretary on a mining asteroid. There'll be another Governor, and if he's not a Bronson client, he'll be someone else's. I'm not supposed to depress you. You've got a decision to make. I've been assigned to a regular Line Regiment as adjutant. The 42nd. It's on Kennicott. Tough duty. Probably a lot of fighting, good opportunities, regular troops. I've got room on the staff. Want to come along? They tell me you'll be fit to move by the time the next ship gets here."

"I'll think about it."

"Do that. You've got a good career ahead of you. Now *you're* the youngest captain in the Fleet. Couldn't swing the Military Star, but you'll get another medal."

"I'll think about it. I have to talk with Kathryn—"

He shrugged. "Certainly, Captain." He grinned and went out.

Captain. Captains may marry, Majors should marry, Colonels must marry—

But that was soldier talk, and I wasn't sure I was a soldier. Strange, I thought. Everyone says I am. I've done well, and I have a great career, and it all seems like a fit of madness. Corporal Brady won't be playing his trumpet any longer because of me. Dangier, wounded but alive, until he volunteered to be an artillery spotter. And all the others, Levine and Lieberman and recruit—no, Private—Dietz, and the rest, dead and blended together in my memory until I can't remember where they died or what for, only that I killed them.

But we won. It was a glorious victory. That was enough for Falkenberg. He had done his job and done it well. Was it enough for me? Would it be in the future?

When I was up and around, I couldn't avoid meeting Governor Swale. Irina was nursing Louis Bonneyman. Louis was worse off than I was. Sometimes they can grow you a new leg, but it takes time, and it's painful. Irina saw him every day, and when I could leave the hospital she insisted that I come to the palace. It was inevitable that I would meet the Governor.

"I hope you're proud of yourself," Swale said. "Everyone else is."

"Hugo, that's not fair," Irina protested.

"Not fair?" Swale said. "How isn't it fair?"

"I did the job I was paid to do, sir," I said.

"Yes. You did, indeed—and thereby made it impossible for me to do mine. Sit down, Captain Slater. Your Major Falkenberg has told you plenty of stories about me. Now let me tell you my side of it."

"There's no need, Governor," I said.

"No, there isn't. Are you afraid to find out just what you've done?"

"No. I've helped throw out a gang of convicts who pretended to be a government. And I'm proud enough of that."

"Are you? Have you been to the Allan Valley lately, Captain? Of course you haven't. And I doubt Kathryn Malcolm has told you what's happening there—how Wan Loo and Harry Seeton and a religious fanatic named Brother Dornan have established commissions of deacons to inquire into the morals and loyalties of everyone in the valley; how anyone they find deficient is turned off the land to make room for their own people. No, I don't suppose she told you any of that."

"I don't believe you."

"Don't you? Ask Miss Malcolm. Or would you believe Irina? She knows it's true."

I looked to Irina. The pain in her eyes was enough. She didn't have to speak.

"I was Governor of the whole planet, Slater. Not just Harmony, not just the Jordan and Allan valleys, but all of the planet. Only they gave me responsibilities and no authority, and no means to govern. What am I supposed to do with the convicts, Slater? They ship them here by the thousands, but they give me nothing to feed them with. You've seen them. How are they supposed to live?"

"They can work—"

"At what? As farmhands on ranches of five hundred hectares? The best land on the planet, doled out as huge ranches with half the land not worked because there's no fertilizer, no irrigation, not even decent drainage systems. They sure as hell can't work in our non-existent industries. Don't you see that Arrarat *must* industrialize? It doesn't matter what

Allan Valley farmers want, or what the other holy Joes want. It's industrialize or face famine, and, by God, there'll be no famines while I can do something about them."

"So you were willing to sell out the 501st. Help the Association defeat us. An honorable way to achieve an honorable end."

"As honorable as yours. Yours is to kill and destroy. War is honorable, but deceit isn't. I prefer my way, Captain."

"I expect you do."

Swale nodded vigorously, to himself, not to me. "Smug. Proud and smug. Tell me, Captain, just how are you better than the Protective Association? They fought. Not for the honor of the corps, but for their land, their families, for friends. They lost. You had better men, better officers, better training. A lot better equipment. If you'd lost, you'd have been returned to Garrison under terms. The Association troops were shot out of hand. All of them. Be proud, Slater. But you make me sick. I'll leave you now. I don't care to argue with my daughter's guests."

"That's true also, isn't it?" I asked Irina. "They shot all the Association troops?"

"Not all," Irina said. "The ones that surrendered to Captain Falkenberg are still alive. He even recruited some of them."

He would. The battalion would need men after those battles. "What's happened to the rest?"

"They're under guard at Beersheba. It was after your Marines left the valley that the real slaughter began."

"Sure. People who wouldn't turn out to fight for their homes when we needed their help got real patriotic after it was over," I said. "I'm going back to my quarters, Irina. Thank you for having me over."

"But Kathryn is coming. She'll be here—"

"I don't want to see anyone just now. Excuse me." I left quickly and wandered through the streets of Harmony. People nodded and smiled as I passed. The Marines were still popular. Of course. We'd opened the trade route up the Jordan, and we'd cleared out the Allan Valley. Grain was cheap, and we'd held the convicts at bay. Why shouldn't the people love us?

Tattoo sounded as I entered the fort. The trumpets and drums sounded through the night, martial and complex and the notes were sweet. Sentries saluted as I passed. Life here was orderly and there was no need to think.

Hartz had left a full bottle of brandy where I could find it. It was his theory that the reason I wasn't healing fast was that I didn't drink enough. The surgeons didn't share his opinion. They were chopping away at me, then using the regeneration stimulators to make me grow better parts. It was a painful process, and they didn't think liquor helped it much.

To hell with them, I thought, and poured a double. I hadn't finished it when Kathryn came in.

"Irina said—Hal, you shouldn't be drinking."

"I doubt that Irina said that."

"You know—what's the matter with you, Hal?"

"Why didn't you tell me?" I asked.

"I was going to. Later. But there never was a right time."

"And it's all true? Your friends are driving the families of everyone who cooperated with the Association out into the hills? And they've shot all the prisoners?"

"It's—yes. It's true."

"Why didn't you stop them?"

"Should I have wanted to?" She looked at the scars on her hands. "Should I?"

There was a knock at the door. "Come in," I said.

It was Falkenberg. "Thought you were alone," he said.

"Come in. I'm confused."

"I expect you are. Got any more of that brandy?"

"Sure. What did you mean by that?"

"I understand you've just learned what's happening out in the Allan Valley."

"Crapdoodle! Has Irina been talking to everyone in Garrison? I don't need a convention of people to cheer me up."

"You don't eh?" He made no move to leave. "Spit it out, Mister."

"You don't call Captains 'Mister.' "

He grinned. "No. Sorry. What's the problem, Hal? Finding out that things aren't as simple as you'd like them to be?"

"John, what the hell were we fighting for out there? What good do we do?"

He stretched a long arm toward the brandy bottle and poured for both of us. "We threw a gang of criminals out. Do you doubt that's what they were? Do you insist that the people we helped be saints?"

"But the women. And children. What will happen to them? And the Governor's right—something's got to be done for the convicts. Poor bastards are sent here, and we can't just drown them."

"There's land to the west," Kathryn said. "They can have that. My grandfather had to start from the beginning. Why can't the new arrivals?"

"The Governor's right about a lot of things," Falkenberg said. "Industry's got to come to Arrarat someday. Should it come just to make the Bronson family rich? At the expense of a bunch of farmers who bought their land with one hell of a lot of hard work and blood? Hal, if you're having second thoughts about the action here on Arrarat, what'll you do when the Fleet's ordered to do something completely raw?"

"I don't know. That's what bothers me."

"You asked what good we do," Falkenberg said. "We buy time. Back on Earth they're ready to start a war that won't end until billions are dead. The Fleet's the only thing preventing that. The only thing, Hal. Be as cynical about the CoDominium as you like. Be contemptuous of Grand Senator Bronson and his friends—yes, and most of his enemies, too, damn it. But remember that the Fleet keeps the peace, and as long as we do, Earth still lives. If the price of that is getting our hands dirty out here on the frontiers, then it's a price we have to pay. And while we're paying it, just once in a while we do something right. I think we did that here. For all that they've been vicious enough now that the battle's over, Wan Loo and his people aren't evil. I'd rather trust the future to them than to people who'd do . . . that." He took Kathryn's hand and turned it over in his. "We can't make things perfect, Hal. But we can damned sure end some of the worst things people do to each other. If that's not enough, we have our own honor, even if our masters have none. The Fleet is our country, Hal, and it's an honorable fatherland." Then he laughed and drained his glass. "Talking's dry work. Pipe Major's learned three new tunes. Come and hear them. You deserve a night in the club, and the drinks are on the battalion. You've friends here, and you've not seen much of them."

He stood, the half smile still on his lips. "Good evening, Hal. Kathryn."

"You're going with him, aren't you?" Kathryn said when he'd closed the door.

"You know I don't care all that much for bagpipes—"

"Don't be flippant with me. He's offered you a place with his new regiment, and you're going to take it."

"I don't know. I've been thinking about it—"

"I know. I didn't before, but I do now. I watched you while he was talking. You're going."

"I guess I am. Will you come with me?"

"If you'll have me, yes. I can't go back to the ranch. I'll have to sell it. I couldn't ever live there now. I'm not the same girl I was when this started."

"I'll always have doubts," I said. "I'll need—" I couldn't finish the thought, but I didn't have to. She came to me, and she wasn't trembling at all, not the way she'd been before, anyway. I held her for a long time.

"We should go now," she said finally. "They'll be expecting you."

"But—"

"We've plenty of time, Hal. A long time."

As we left the room, Last Post sounded across the fort.

HE'S OPINIONATED

HE'S DYNAMIC

HE'S LARGER THAN LIFE

MARTIN CAIDIN

Martin Caidin is a bestselling novelist, pilot *extraordinaire*, and expert on America's space program. *He's also a prophet of technological change.* His ability to predict future trends verges on the psychic, as when he wrote *Cyborg* (the novel which became "The Six Million Dollar Man") and *Marooned* (which precipitated the American-Soviet Apollo-Soyuz linkup mission). His tense, action-filled stories are based on personal experience in fields such as astronautics, aviation, oceanography and the military.

Caidin's characters also know their stuff. And they take on real life, because they're based on real people. Martin Caidin spent a stint as a merchant seaman in Europe and Africa, worked for Air Force Intelligence in the U.S. and Asia, and has flown his own planes to many parts of the world. His adventures can be yours in these novels from Baen Books.

— — — — — — — — — — — — —

EXIT EARTH—Just as the US and the USSR have finally settled their differences, American scientists discover that the solar system is about to pass through a cloud of cosmic dust that will incite the Sun to a paroxysm of fury. All will die. There can be no escape—except, possibly, for a very few. *This is their story.* 656 pp. • 65630-9 • $4.50 _____

KILLER STATION—Earth's first space station *Pleiades* is a scientific boon—until one brief moment of sabotage changes it into a terrible Sword of Damocles. 55996-6 • 384 pp. • $3.50 _____

THE MESSIAH STONE—"An unusual thriller . . . not only in subject matter, but in the fact that the author claims that the basic idea behind the book is real! [THE MESSIAH STONE] concerns the possession of a stone; the person who controls the stone rules the world. The last such person is rumored to be Adolf Hitler. . . . Harrowing adventure and nonstop action."—*Science Fiction Review.* 65562-0 • 416 pp. • $3.95 _____

ZOBOA—It started with the hijacking of four atomic bombs, and ended with the Space Shuttle atop a pillar of fire. . . . "From the marvelous, cinematic opening pages, Caidin sweeps the reader along in a raucous, exciting thriller."—*Publishers Weekly* 65588-4 • 448 pp. • $3.50 _____

To order these Baen Books, check each title selected and return with a check or money order for the combined cover price. Send to Baen Books, 260 Fifth Avenue, New York, N.Y. 10001.

Distributed by Simon & Schuster
1230 Avenue of the Americas • New York, N.Y. 10020